'I don't bite, Sarah, despite what you so obviously think.'

'What?' She turned and stared at him with huge shocked eyes, wondering if she'd imagined that dry note of humour in his voice. Humour and Niall Gillespie? Never! They were a contradiction in terms!

He gave the softest laugh imaginable, yet Sarah felt every cell in her body bask in the sensation of warmth it left behind.

'I said I don't bite. Are you prepared to take my word for it, Sarah? Or do you want me to get an affidavit to that effect?'

Jennifer Taylor lives in the north-west of England with her husband Bill and children Mark and Vicky. She had been writing Mills & Boon® romances for some years, but when she discovered Medical Romances™, she was so captivated by these heart-warming stories that she set out to write them herself! When not writing or doing research for her latest book, Jennifer's hobbies include reading, travel, walking her dog and retail therapy (shopping!). Jennifer claims all that bending and stretching to reach the shelves is the best exercise possible. It definitely beats step aerobics...

Recent titles by the same author:

THE HUSBAND SHE NEEDS*
HOME AT LAST*
OUR NEW MUMMY*
MARRYING HER PARTNER*

Country Practice Quartet

TENDER LOVING CARE

BY
JENNIFER TAYLOR

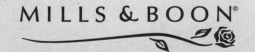

First published in Great Britain 2000
Harlequin Mills & Boon Limited,
Eton House, 18-24 Paradise Road, Richmond, Surrey TW9 1SR

© Jennifer Taylor 2000

ISBN 0 263 82231 1

Set in Times Roman 10½ on 12 pt.
03-0004-47203

Printed and bound in Spain
by Litografia Rosés, S.A., Barcelona

CHAPTER ONE

'AND that makes one hundred and twenty-nine!' Staff Nurse Sarah Harris announced as she came into the staffroom. Going straight to the notice-board, she wrote the new total next to her name then grinned. 'Mrs Peters...twins,' she explained succinctly.

'Typical! I might have known you'd get a double.' Irene Prentice, senior midwife on the unit, rolled her eyes. 'What do you do to your mums, Sarah, bribe them? You won last year's competition for delivering the most babies, and it looks as though you're going to win this year, too!'

'You're a fine one to talk. One of your mums produced triplets last week, so I don't know how you can begrudge me a little bonus!' Sarah laughed as she plugged in the kettle and made herself a cup of coffee. She plonked herself down into a chair and kicked off her shoes with a sigh of relief.

'Oh, does that feel good! I think I'm almost as exhausted as Mrs Peters is. She was absolutely marvellous and did everything we asked her to, but her husband was a terrified, poor man. I honestly thought he was going to pass out at one point. We ended up giving him a whiff of gas and air to quieten his nerves!'

Irene laughed as she got up. 'It takes a lot of fathers that way. Wait till you've seen as many as

I have sprawled across the delivery-room floor. Still at least he was there and that counts for a lot.' She smiled reminiscently as she washed her cup.

'When I first became a midwife it wasn't the done thing for the dads to be present at the birth. I remember the matron at the first hospital I worked in complaining bitterly because one poor man had dared to ask if he could be with his wife. Things have changed a lot since those days, thank heavens!'

'I should say so. Now it's rare if the father isn't present.' Sarah sipped her coffee. 'Are you still thinking about retiring, Irene? Sure you won't regret it? I can't imagine giving all this up. I enjoy the job too much!'

'I know you do. And that's why you're so good at it. A good midwife needs to be both patient and firm, and you manage to be both. All your mums say the same thing, that they don't know how they would have coped without you.' Irene smiled as she dried her hands. 'I used to feel the same, Sarah. But lately I just feel that I'd like more free time now that Jack's finished work, so that we can do all the things we promised ourselves we'd do.'

'I understand, of course. It's just such a shame that you'll be leaving so soon after Dr Henderson had to retire.' Sarah sighed. 'Things aren't going to be the same around here.'

'No, probably not. Although from what I've heard this Niall Gillespie who's taking over is very highly thought of. But, of course, he's bound to have his own ideas about how things should be done. Mind you, now that the area health authority has decided to close the maternity wards at the Royal and make Dalverston General a centre of excellence for obstetric care, things were bound to change.'

'I know that. And don't get me wrong—I think it's wonderful that we'll get all the equipment we need so desperately at last. Oh, I know there's been a lot of hoo-ha in the papers about the closure, but with the two hospitals being only ten miles apart it makes sense to make the best use possible of resources,' she said quickly.

'But?' Irene queried. 'I get the feeling that you have reservations despite what you just said.'

'Well, I suppose I have in a way.' Sarah shrugged. 'I just don't want to see this place go the way of so many other large maternity units, all high-tech and no soul. Giving birth should be a wonderful experience for a woman. She shouldn't be pressed into the sort of delivery she doesn't want just because it's more convenient for the staff.'

'What makes you think that's going to happen here?' Irene frowned. 'I hope it doesn't, mind you.'

'Oh, it's probably just me being silly.' Sarah got up to wash her cup. 'I've loved every minute of working here so I can't bear the thought that things are going to change at all. I'm just keeping my fingers crossed that this new man isn't going to try to stamp his authority on the place. I've heard that he's a stickler for having things done his way. Let's just hope *his* way fits in with ours!'

She laughed as she turned round then felt the smile freeze on her lips as her eyes clashed with a pair of cool green ones that were watching her from the doorway. She took a quick breath, wondering if it was the shock of discovering that someone was listening to their conversation which made her feel breathless all of a sudden.

Obviously sensing something amiss, Irene also glanced round and she, too, looked surprised to see the newcomer. However, before either of them could say anything, the door was pushed wide open and Elaine Roberts, the hospital manager, came into the room.

'Ah, Sister Prentice, I'm glad I caught you. And you, too, Staff Nurse Harris. I'm just showing Dr Gillespie around and introducing him to as many people as possible.' Elaine smiled at the man who had followed her into the room. 'Sister Prentice is our longest-serving member of staff on the maternity wing, Niall. How many years is it now, Irene? Twenty?'

'Twenty-two, actually,' Irene said pleasantly as she held out her hand. 'Nice to meet you, Dr Gillespie.'

'And you too, Sister Prentice. That's some track record you have. There can't be too many people who've stayed in the job for that length of time.'

His voice was very deep, the faintest hint of a Scottish accent lending an extra richness to its velvety tones. Sarah felt a shiver dance down her spine as she heard it for the first time. She took another quick breath, wondering why her heart seemed to be racing all of a sudden. All right, so it *had* been a surprise to see him standing there, but could that really explain how she felt right then, her nerves taut as bowstrings, her pulse tapping away like Morse-code signals gone crazy?

'And how long have you been here, Staff Nurse?'

She started as she realised he was addressing her, feeling the colour rush to her face as she looked up to find those cool green eyes resting on her. Her tongue suddenly felt too big for her mouth as she tried to answer the simple question.

'Three—al-almost three years,' she stammered.

'I see. And do you enjoy working here?' He folded his arms as he regarded her levelly yet Sarah sensed a deeper intent behind the seemingly innocent question. She took another quick breath as she strove to get her thoughts into order but it was surprisingly difficult. What was it about him that disturbed her so?

In a fast sweep her eyes ran over him while she tried to work out what it was about Dr Niall Gillespie that she found so unsettling. He was tall, she noted, a little over six feet by her estimation, his body lean and fit-looking beneath that immaculate charcoal-grey suit he was wearing with a spotless white shirt. His dark brown hair was neatly cut and brushed smoothly back from his face, emphasising the strong bone structure—high cheek-bones and a ruggedly square jaw, a nose with just the hint of a crook in it.

Sarah frowned as she continued her rapid scrutiny, finding nothing about his appearance to explain her strange reaction. It was a pleasant enough face—indeed, some might have said it was handsome, although his skin was a shade too pale, as though he spent very little time out of doors.

His eyes were his best feature, though, she decided, a shimmering sea green which appeared almost transparent at first glance. It was only as she looked closer that she realised it was impossible to tell what he was thinking from looking into them.

Here was a man who hid his feelings, she thought suddenly, a man who had learned to look at the world with seeming openness yet give nothing of himself away. It made her wonder what he was afraid of people finding out. It was only as she saw his dark brows rise that she realised he was still waiting for her to answer his question.

'Oh, very much, thank you, Dr Gillespie,' she murmured hastily, faintly embarrassed by her own behaviour. 'I love working at Dalverston General.'

'Then let's hope that you don't find any changes I may feel it necessary to make too difficult to adjust to.' He gave her a last cool look then turned to Elaine Roberts. 'You mentioned something about the prem. unit next, I believe?'

'Ah, yes.' Elaine managed a smile but even she looked a little disconcerted. However, it was nothing to how Sarah felt.

'I think I was just well and truly put in my place, don't you?' she said in annoyance as the staffroom door closed behind their visitors.

Irene grimaced. 'Sounded like it. I hope it isn't an indication of how things are going to be around here in the future. If so, I'm glad I'm leaving!'

'I don't blame you. Talk about getting off on the wrong foot...!' she sighed heavily. 'Looks as though I'm going to have to watch what I say in future, doesn't it?'

Irene burst out laughing. 'Fat chance of that! When have you ever thought twice about airing your views, Sarah Harris?'

'Are you trying to say that I'm outspoken or something?' Sarah demanded, laughing despite her chagrin at the way Dr Gillespie had rebuked her in that passionless manner. Was that why it had stung so much, the fact that he'd spoken to her without betraying a shred of emotion? She wasn't sure.

'"Or something" being the operative words!' Irene retorted as she headed for the door. 'Right, I'm off back to see how Mrs Walters is getting on. I'll see you later. You are going to Dr Henderson's retirement do tonight, I take it?'

'I am indeed. I'll see you there, I expect.' Sarah watched Irene leave then sighed as she went and slipped her shoes back on.

She'd been so happy since she'd moved to the small Lancashire town of Dalverston. Maybe she should try to curb her tongue now that the new head of department had made it plain he didn't welcome any opposition. It wasn't worth putting her job on the line…was it?

She straightened abruptly and caught a glimpse of herself in the mirror by the lockers. She shook back her silky blonde hair, her pertly pretty features settling into unaccustomed grim lines, the light of battle flaring in her hazel eyes.

Maybe it wouldn't do her any favours but if she thought something was wrong then she was going to say so! As far as she was concerned, the welfare of her patients came first and foremost. Everything else—including Dr Ice-Man Gillespie—came a very lowly second!

'Good, you're doing brilliantly, Karen. Your cervix is fully dilated. It won't be long now.' Sarah wiped the perspiration from the young woman's face and smiled encouragingly at her.

'I don't think this baby will ever come...' Karen bit her lip as another contraction racked her tired body. Sarah bent down, experiencing the small rush of pleasure she always felt as the baby's head emerged. Gently, she checked that the cord wasn't wrapped around the child's neck then spoke quietly to Helen Court, the trainee midwife who was assisting at the birth.

'Everything is fine. The baby's head rotates in the birth canal, which is why he's facing downwards now. Always make certain that the cord isn't in the way when the head appears. That's most important.'

Helen nodded, gently feeling around the child's neck as Sarah had done. 'Yes, I understand. So what happens next?'

Sarah smiled as she looked at Karen. 'Now we let Mum get on with the job! Now, remember what you were taught at antenatal class, Karen—wait until you feel a contraction, before trying to push. That way you won't exhaust yourself.'

Karen nodded tiredly. She glanced at her husband and managed a smile. 'Not long now, David.'

'You're doing brilliantly! I can't believe it...' David winced when Karen gripped his hand as another contraction began.

Sarah bent to the task of helping the baby make the final part of its journey, quietly pointing out to Helen things she needed to know. 'See how the baby's head has turned again so that it's in line with its shoulders. I'm just going to ease the head down a bit so that the shoulder nearest to the front comes out first... Ah-h, here it comes!'

She deftly lifted the tiny body as it slithered free, laughing as the baby immediately began to wail, its face puckering with annoyance at being so summarily pushed out into the world. 'Don't think much of that, do you, poppet? Never mind, it gets better from here on in.'

She laid the baby gently on its mother's tummy, smiling as she saw the joy on the young couple's faces. 'You have a daughter. Congratulations both of you.'

'A girl? But...but I thought it was going to be a boy!' The new father gulped as he stared in awe at the tiny scrap of humanity that was going to change his whole life.

Karen laughed through her tears as she tenderly stroked the baby's sticky, wet head. 'I told you not to jump the gun by buying those football boots!'

Everyone laughed, then Sarah got on with the last remaining task of delivering the placenta. She carefully checked to make sure there were no bits of it missing, which could cause infection if they were left inside the mother, then quietly drew Helen aside to give the new parents these first precious moments alone together with their child.

'We'll do all the necessary bits and pieces in a few moments. The baby will need to be weighed and measured, then checked for things like displaced hips. You know what the Apgar test is, don't you?'

Helen nodded. 'I think so. It's a sort of scoring system to assess the baby's physical condition, isn't it?'

'That's right. It's done simply by observing the baby's breathing, skin colour, muscle tone and general vitality then awarding points for each. The highest number of points a baby can get is ten but we're quite happy so long as it scores more than seven. We do it as soon as the child is born and then again a few minutes later.

'However, when the birth has been as straightforward as this one was, I always try to let the parents have a few quiet moments with their child before we whisk it away. The tests are essential, of course, but a lot of mothers find it distressing to be parted from their baby almost before they've had chance to look at it.'

She glanced round as the door suddenly opened and was surprised to see Dr Gillespie coming into the delivery room. He was wearing a green scrub suit now and had a stethoscope looped around his neck. He nodded to the young couple then came over to her.

'Everything all right here, Staff Nurse Harris?'

'Fine, thank you, sir.' Sarah matched her tone to his—or tried to, at least. It wasn't easy to inject the same degree of coolness into her voice that Niall Gillespie managed to do!

She clamped down on an unaccustomed irritation as she introduced Helen to the new chief of obstetrics, then quietly instructed the student to prepare the identity tags with which each baby was fitted before leaving the delivery room.

Dr Gillespie waited while Sarah explained the procedure, his expression as aloof as ever as he listened. It made her feel incredibly self-conscious to have him there, listening to—and probably judging—every word she said, but she tried not to let it show.

Having satisfied herself that Helen understood just how important the tags were, she turned back to Niall Gillespie, wondering what he wanted. 'Are you still familiarising yourself with the unit, then, Doctor?' she enquired politely.

'Oh, I think I have a pretty fair idea of where everything is now, thank you, Staff.' He gave her a thin smile, before glancing towards the couple, who were oblivious to everything except their child. 'Have all the necessary checks been done?'

It was a pointless question because he could see very clearly that they hadn't. Sarah was immediately on the defensive, although she had no idea why she should be because she hadn't done anything wrong. 'Not yet. I like to give the parents a few moments alone with their child before I take it away.'

'And is that the usual procedure?'

His tone was as impersonal as ever so there was no excuse for the sudden annoyance she felt. She looked directly at him, feeling the quiver which ran through her as her eyes locked with those cool green ones which gave so little away. 'It's something *I* always do when the birth is as uncomplicated as this one was, Doctor. I find that the parents value this time more than any other. It's a chance for them to adjust to the idea that their baby is a reality at long last.'

'A touching sentiment, Staff. However, I consider it both foolish and unnecessary to take any risks with the health of either mother or child. In future, please, ensure that everything is done strictly by the book and that both mother and baby are thoroughly examined to avoid any complications arising.'

He turned to leave but Sarah was so incensed by his attitude that she reached out and stopped him. 'There were no risks to either the mother or the child, I assure you!'

'None that were apparent, perhaps.' He gave her a glacial smile before his eyes dropped pointedly to where her hand was resting on his arm.

She let it fall to her side, embarrassed colour rushing to her face as she realised what she had done. She could feel its heat burning her cheeks and was mortified that she couldn't control it. It was the bane of her life—if she was angry or aroused in any way it showed in her face. And it didn't help to realise that it was such a betraying indication of her feelings to Niall Gillespie!

She took a quick breath, striving to flatten all inflection from her voice because she hated him knowing that he'd upset her. 'I imagine that I've delivered enough babies by now, Doctor, to be able to assess when either a mother or a child is at risk.'

'Perhaps. But in future, Staff, I would prefer it if you followed the guidelines to the letter.' His voice dropped so that his accent seemed more pronounced all of a sudden. Sarah wondered if it was that which seemed to imbue the rich tones with a wealth of emotion that tugged at her heartstrings. 'The unexpected can always happen. That is something we all must be aware of. We cannot afford to take *any* unnecessary risks.'

He turned to leave then paused and glanced back. 'By the way, what is it?'

'What is it...?' she repeated inanely, trying to decide if her imagination had been playing tricks. Niall Gillespie looked as cool and remote as ever; there was nothing about his demeanor to even hint at that anguished note she'd heard for a moment in his voice.

'The baby? Is it a boy or a girl?' he prompted her, and she dragged her thoughts back into line.

'Oh, a girl.' She glanced at the whiteboard where she'd written the names the parents had chosen. 'Holly Louise, I believe she's going to be called.'

'Then please give the parents my congratulations.' He didn't say anything more, merely closed the delivery room door quietly behind him as he left.

Sarah stared after him for a few seconds before Karen called her. She went over to the bed and answered the new mother's questions about the creamy substances called vernix which coated the baby's skin. However, all the time she was explaining its purpose to the fascinated parents, her mind was only partly on what she was saying.

Had she imagined it? she wondered again as she took the baby over to the scales to weigh her. Or had she *really* heard that note of pain in Niall Gillespie's voice just now?

She couldn't decide and that was the trouble. If she'd been able to dismiss it as pure imagination then that would have been the end of it. Now Sarah knew that her curiosity had been thoroughly aroused…although she doubted that Niall Gillespie would appreciate her interest!

CHAPTER TWO

'SARAH...over here! We've saved you a seat.'

'Thanks. I thought I was never going to get here! The bus didn't come so I had to go back home and ring for a taxi.'

Sarah squeezed into the gap next to Irene and smiled round at the assembled group. Quite a crowd had gathered in the pub next to the hospital to have a drink before they all moved on to Dr Henderson's retirement party, which was being held in a nearby hotel. There were staff there from many different departments as well as the maternity unit, she realised.

'My, my, I hardly recognised you lot. You all look so glamorous out of uniform!' she quipped.

Everyone laughed then Helen picked up her glass and raised it aloft. 'How about a toast to my very first delivery—to baby Holly Louise, the first of many!'

'Holly Louise!' everyone chorused. Sarah glanced round as someone thrust a glass into her hand.

'Here, have this to wet the baby's head.'

'Thanks, Mike.' Sarah smiled at Mike Dawson, who had recently been appointed to the post of junior houseman on the surgical ward. She took a sip of shandy then raised her voice to carry above the din the others were making. 'I thought you were on duty tonight?'

'I am. Can't you tell?' Mike grimaced as he held up a glass of orange squash. 'I thought I'd pop over while I was on my break to see how you're fixed for tomorrow night. Fancy going to see that new film they've got on at the Ritz? You'll be on nights in a couple of days so we'll miss it if we don't go soon.'

'Sure.' Sarah agreed readily enough, although she wasn't deaf to the eagerness with which Mike made the arrangements to pick her up the following evening. He had to leave shortly after that, laughing as everyone teased him about having to work while they all enjoyed themselves. She gave him a wave when he reached the door, inwardly sighing as she wondered if he was getting a bit too attached to her.

'Looks smitten to me. Are those wedding bells I can hear in the distance?' Irene whispered, giving her an old-fashioned look.

Sarah laughed. 'I doubt it! Your trouble, Irene Prentice, is that you're an incurable romantic. Just because you've had thirty years of wedded bliss you want to see everyone else go the same way.'

'I can't deny it.' Irene shrugged, not at all put out by the pithy comment. 'Mike's a nice boy, Sarah. And he's obviously taken with you.'

'Hmm, that's as may be. However, it takes two to tango, Irene, or so they say.'

'Meaning that you're not interested in him in that way?' Irene sighed regretfully. 'Pity. Your trouble,

Sarah is that you're just too choosy. At this rate
you'll never find the perfect man.'

'Then I'll just have to do without, won't I?'
Sarah laughed as she picked up her glass, although
she knew there was more than a grain of truth in
what Irene had said. She *was* choosy and she made
no apology for it. Oh, she'd been out with a lot of
different men but she'd never found anyone she'd
felt she could spend her whole life with, and that
included Mike! It didn't worry her unduly because
she was confident that one day she would find the
one man who would make her life complete.

She took another sip of her drink as she tried to
picture him. Would he be dark or fair, tall or short?

The vague image which had been forming began
to take on substance and she coughed as a mouthful
of shandy shot down the wrong way. Suddenly, all
she could see was a pair of green eyes—sea-green
eyes—under jet-black brows, staring at her...

'Ready?' Irene jogged her elbow to warn her
they were ready to leave for the party, and Sarah
hastily drew a veil over the picture in her head. She
glanced at the remains of the shandy then pushed
the glass away. There had to be a reason why Niall
Gillespie had popped into her mind just then and
the shandy must have been to blame for painting
him, Dr Ice himself, in the guise of the perfect man!

'I just want to thank you all very much for this
wonderful present.' Dr Henderson smiled as he held
up the fishing rod the staff had bought him. 'Every
time I use it I'll think of you!'

Everyone clapped as the elderly doctor was

helped down from the chair he'd been using as a podium. He made his way back to the alcove by the French windows where a number of drinks were lined up on a ledge. Giving Sarah a rueful smile, he bypassed the glasses of whisky and picked up a tumbler of mineral water.

'I never realised before how hard it is to follow doctor's orders. I'd give anything for a nip of whisky but Meg will have my guts for garters if I get home smelling of the stuff!'

Sarah laughed. 'She's only thinking of you, Dr Henderson.'

'I know, I know,' he sighed. 'And I'm going to be sensible, Sarah. That heart attack I had was a warning I intend to heed. From now on I mean to do everything by the book!'

Sarah frowned as the older man used the very phrase Niall Gillespie had used that afternoon. She glanced round and immediately spotted him at the far side of the room. It was odd how she seemed able to home in on him like that, as though she had some sort of inbuilt radar. Several times during the evening when her thoughts had strayed to him she had looked up and there he'd been, directly in her line of sight...

He suddenly glanced round, his brows drawing together as he found her looking at him. Sarah felt the colour rush to her face and turned away, embarrassed to be caught staring like that. She forced herself to concentrate on what Dr Henderson was saying as he outlined his plans for a fishing holiday in Scotland, yet she could feel the skin on the back of her neck prickling in the strangest way...

'I can recommend a few good places to try that rod out, Richard.'

She started nervously as she recognised the deep voice which spoke directly behind her. A few drops of wine slopped over the side of her glass and she felt the colour rise to her cheeks again as saw Niall Gillespie glance at her. She looked round for some-where to put her glass while she wiped her wet fingers then jumped again as a large hand lifted it out of her grasp.

'Allow me, Staff Nurse Harris.' Niall Gillespie smiled coolly as she murmured her thanks. Hur-riedly opening her bag, she rummaged through it for a tissue, aware that he was watching her with that same chilly smile on his lips.

It made her deeply self-conscious to be the object of his scrutiny so that suddenly she was all fingers and thumbs, fumbling so much that she managed to spill half the contents of her bag. Two lipsticks, a pair of earrings and a handful of loose change scattered across the floor and ended up under a nearby table.

Sarah's face flamed with mortification as she crouched down to retrieve them. What on earth was the matter with her? She was acting like some sort of…moonstruck teenager, fumbling and dropping things just because Dr Ice had condescended to hold her drink!

On hands and knees, she scrabbled about under the table, gathering up her belongings, then nearly jumped out of her skin as a face appeared at the other side of it. She felt her heart give one small lurch and then a second before it was off and running like crazy, making it impossible for her to think of anything to say. It was left to Niall Gillespie to save the day and he did that in his most impersonal tone.

'I believe one of those lipsticks went under the bench over there… Ah, I can see it now!'

He retrieved the lipstick then stood up. Sarah closed her eyes and counted to ten, hoping to get herself back if not on a completely even keel then at least on one that didn't wobble so much! It was another mistake, she quickly discovered. Suddenly all she could see were those sea-green eyes staring at her from the other side of the table. It reminded her rather too sharply of what had happened in the pub earlier, and how her poor shandy-soaked mind had conjured up Niall Gillespie as the answer to her dreams…

She bit back a slightly hysterical laugh as she rose to her feet with as much dignity as she could muster in the circumstances. It was a good job she'd refused any more alcoholic drinks that night. There was no knowing what other little fantasies her mind might come up with!

'Here you are.'

Niall Gillespie held out his hand, the tube of lipstick nestling in his large palm. Sarah took it from him with a murmur of thanks, trying to ignore the tremor that ran through her as her fingertips brushed his palm. She popped the lipstick back into her bag then fixed a smile to her mouth as she strove to edit out all awareness of his presence, but that was like trying not to be aware of the sun shining!

She could feel the heat from his body through

the thin fabric of her pale green dress, feel the way goose-bumps rose on her bare arms, feel how her nipples suddenly started to tauten...

Sarah just managed to bite back a gasp of dismay as she realised what was happening. It stunned her, shocked her, horrified her. What was the matter with her? Why on earth should she find this man's nearness a turn-on?

She rushed into speech, not wanting to give herself time to think about that. 'Do you fish, then, Dr Gillespie?'

'I used to.' He gave her another of those cool smiles but she fancied that it wasn't quite so cool as it had been. There seemed to be a definite hint of strain around his mouth now, a certain tension about the way he stood there, his gaze focused on a spot just above her head. It was a relief when Dr Henderson picked up the conversation and offered a much-needed distraction.

'It's difficult to find the time for hobbies, isn't it, Niall? You get so caught up in the job that everything else takes second place.' Dr Henderson sighed regretfully. 'I wish now that I'd had the sense to get a bit more balance in my life, then the prospect of retirement wouldn't seem quite so daunting. Still, there's no point in looking back. It's the future I have to think about now. And if I don't get myself home soon I'll have Meg after me!'

Dr Henderson turned to Sarah with a smile. 'I believe you had trouble getting here tonight, Sarah. Would you like to share a taxi with me? I could drop you off on my way home.'

'Oh, yes, please. If you're sure it isn't any trouble.' She leapt at the offer. Not only was it the perfect excuse to leave but it would save her having to dip into next week's housekeeping to pay another expensive taxi fare. 'I'll just go and tell the others I'm leaving then I'll meet you outside, Dr Henderson.'

She hurried off, quickly explaining to Irene what she intended to do. A couple of people tried to persuade her to stay but she pleaded tiredness as her excuse for leaving so early. And maybe it wasn't such a trumped-up excuse after all, she mused as she made her way from the room. The shift had been a particularly busy one. Apart from the twins and Holly Louise, there had been three other births as well.

Perhaps that explained the other odd things that had happened tonight, she thought with a sudden flash of inspiration. Like the way she had reacted to Niall Gillespie's nearness just now. Her system had just about reached overload so was it any wonder that signals were getting crossed?

Pleased to have found such a rational explanation, she made her way to the hotel's foyer, but there was no sign of Dr Henderson. She went out to the front steps, wondering if she should hail a taxi if she saw one. There weren't all that many cabs in the town, especially not at this time of night. It would be a shame to let one pass and then have to wait ages for another to turn up.

She went down into the street, shivering a little as the night air struck her bare arms. She hadn't bothered with a coat as it had been a warm evening, an Indian summer having set in a few days earlier.

Now, as she felt the chill of the night air, she wished she'd thought to bring a jacket with her.

'You're going to catch your death, standing there like that. Come along.'

She swung round, her eyes widening as she found Niall Gillespie behind her. He gave her a cool smile and nodded to where a car was parked across the road. 'I told Richard I'd give you both a lift. There's no point waiting around for a taxi when I'm going that way.'

'Oh, but I couldn't…I mean it isn't necessary…' She took a quick breath to control her racing heartbeat. 'What I'm trying to say is that you don't have to give me a lift, Dr Gillespie. I'll get a taxi.'

She half turned away then stopped as he said softly, 'I don't bite, Sarah, despite what you so obviously think.'

'What?' She turned and stared at him with huge shocked eyes, wondering if she'd imagined that dry note of humour in his voice. Humour and Niall Gillespie? Never! They were a contradiction in terms!

He gave the softest laugh imaginable, yet Sarah felt every cell in her body bask in the sensation of warmth it left behind.

'I said I don't bite. Are you prepared to take my word for it, Sarah? Or do you want me to get an affidavit to that effect?'

'I…' She gave a choked laugh, her own sense of humour suddenly rising to the occasion. 'Oh, nothing less than an affidavit! I mean, a girl can't be too careful, especially not on a night like this,' she added, looking pointedly up at the sky.

Niall followed her gaze and laughed throatily. 'Mmm, I see what you mean. A full moon tonight, is it? Still, I'm sure you're prepared for every eventuality, Staff Nurse Harris. I imagine that, along with all the other *essential* paraphernalia you've managed to pack into that bag, you have the requisite silver bullet. That *is* the recommended method of dealing with a werewolf, isn't it? I must confess that my knowledge of such things is somewhat limited.'

'Oh, dear! I didn't think to bring it with me tonight,' she answered, wondering a little wildly if they were *really* having this conversation. If anyone had told her half an hour ago that this would be happening she would have laughed!

She gave herself a pinch just in case she was dreaming, but Niall Gillespie was still standing there, a faintly self-conscious smile playing about his beautiful mouth...

She took a quick breath, wondering exactly *when* she'd realised that his mouth was beautiful, then decided hurriedly that she didn't want to know the answer to that question! It was a relief when Dr Henderson appeared, surrounded by most of the maternity unit staff who had come to wave him off. He came down the steps to join them and smiled at Sarah.

'Niall's told you that he'd offered us a lift home, has he, my dear? Good, good.'

He didn't wait for her to reply, turning to give one last wave to the crowd gathered on the steps who were now cheering noisily. Sarah quickly slid into the back seat of the car after Niall had unlocked the doors, trying to ignore the speculative looks being cast her way. She didn't need to see them to know that she was going to have a lot of explaining to do the following day!

'So, did you invite him in for coffee, then, Sarah? And how long did he stay?'

'I didn't and he didn't. Does that answer your questions?' Sarah sighed heavily as she headed for the door. I'm going through to Reception if anyone wants me.'

'Oh, don't worry, if *Niall* comes looking for you we'll tell him where to find you!'

Sally Green, one of the midwives on Sarah's shift, burst into peals of laughter. Sarah ignored her as she left the staffroom but it wasn't easy. She'd been teased endlessly since she'd come on duty that morning!

News about Niall Gillespie giving her a lift home had spread like wildfire through the department, probably even through the whole of the hospital. Everyone had wanted to know what had happened, and yet when she'd tried to tell them they'd refused to believe her. She could go on repeating herself until she was blue in the face but nobody would accept that Niall Gillespie had simply driven her home and that had been all!

Sarah smiled wryly as she thought about the night before. It had taken all of sixty seconds for Niall to stop the car and get out to open her door for her. She'd been a little surprised by that small courtesy as, in her experience, most men didn't bother with such things nowadays. But Niall had got out and opened the door for her, had even taken her hand to help her...

She shivered as she suddenly recalled just how warm and firm his fingers had felt as they'd closed around hers, and how long the imprint of them had lingered afterwards. All the time she'd been getting ready for bed she'd been able to feel it, so that once she'd actually found herself staring at her hand as though she might find some physical evidence of his touch!

There had been nothing there, of course, and she'd laughed at her own foolishness as she'd got into bed and turned off the lights. It had just been another indication of how tired she'd been.

She'd fallen asleep on that thought, happy to have found such a simple explanation for everything that had happened. Nevertheless, as she reached the reception area and spotted Niall Gillespie standing by the check-in desk she couldn't deny the tremor that ran through her body and seemed to make a mockery of all her reasoning.

However she tried to explain it, there was no denying that Niall Gillespie did possess a strange ability to disturb her equilibrium!

'Ah, Staff Nurse Harris, come with me, please. I want you to assist me this morning, if you would.' His tone was clipped to the point of brusqueness when he turned and saw her. Sarah smoothed her face into an expressionless mask, praying that he wouldn't guess how disturbed she felt by the announcement.

'Sister Prentice usually assists Dr Henderson at

antenatal clinic, Dr Gillespie,' she said with a calmness she was far from feeling.

'So I believe.' His brows drew together as he picked up a stack of manila folders and came over to her. 'However, in view of the fact that Sister Prentice will be retiring shortly I think it would be far less disruptive this way. There's little point in training Sister Prentice to my way of doing things only to have her leave. Staff Nurse Bradshaw will be assisting Dr Patel from now on and you'll assist me.'

'Of course, Doctor,' Sarah concurred quietly, taking a deep breath she followed him to the examination cubicles. It made sense, of course, because she knew how much easier it was for a woman if she was able to see the same midwife and doctor each time she came for an appointment. She was able to build up a rapport with the staff and usually found it easier to confide any worries she had to someone she knew.

Continuity of care was something that Sarah believed in wholeheartedly, although Dr Henderson had taken a far more relaxed view, picking and choosing which patients he'd see on clinic days. She agreed with Niall Gillespie's decision yet the thought of working in such close proximity with him over the coming weeks was rather unsettling.

Determined not to let him know that, however, Sarah concentrated on her work as they made their way through the list of mothers due to see a specialist that morning. There were three new mums, each of them nervous and unsure about what was happening and why. Niall Gillespie was marvellous with them, calm and patient as he explained why antenatal care was so essential to their well-being and to that of their unborn babies.

'You may have wondered why the nurse you saw when you arrived needed to take some blood from you.' Niall sat on the edge of the couch and smiled at Hannah Jarvis, one of the new mums who seemed especially tense. 'There are a number of things we need to test for, so we'll take a blood sample each time you come so that we can check you aren't becoming anaemic and so on. What we need to know straight away is which blood group you are and whether you are Rhesus—negative.'

'What does that mean, Doctor? Is it a disease?' Hannah frowned, although Sarah could see that she was starting to relax a little as she listened to what he was telling her.

He shook his head. 'No, it isn't a disease. Most people are Rhesus-positive but a certain percentage of the population are negative, which causes them no problems at all normally. However, if you are Rhesus-negative then it's essential that we know that because it could have implications for the baby's health.'

'In what way?' Hannah asked curiously.

'If the baby is Rhesus-negative, like its mother, there isn't a problem, but if it's Rhesus-positive then it could become very anaemic and we would need to monitor its progress very carefully. However, the main cause for concern is if any of the baby's blood cells leaked into your bloodstream during the birth. If that happened your body would start manufacturing antibodies to fight the Rhesus factor those blood cells contain.

'The danger then is that during a subsequent pregnancy those antibodies would pass through the placenta and attack another Rhesus-positive baby's blood. And that can lead to all sorts of things such as jaundice, severe anaemia or even brain damage in the unborn child.'

'Good heavens! But can nothing be done about it? Or are you saying that a Rhesus-negative woman shouldn't risk having a second child?' Hannah frowned at the idea.

'Not at all. It's simply a question of giving the mother an injection of serum which stops antibodies forming after each delivery. Then there's no risk to the next child she has, although each subsequent pregnancy would be closely monitored, of course.'

'It's fantastic what you can do, Doctor. I must say, I couldn't understand why the nurse needed to do a blood test. I've always been scared of needles but now I know what it's for I don't mind so much.' Hannah pressed a hand to her barely discernible bump. 'If it's to make sure the baby is safe then it's worth it, isn't it?'

Niall's smile lit up his whole face as he got up and patted the young mother's hand. 'It is. It's a small price to pay for a healthy child. Now, Staff Nurse Harris will help you get comfortable before I examine you. If there's anything you want to know, Mrs Jarvis, please, ask. The more you know about what's going on the easier it will be for you. I'll be back in a few seconds.'

He left the cubicle, leaving Sarah to get the

young mother settled on the couch for the examination every woman had on her first visit to the clinic. She draped a sheet over Hannah Jarvis, knowing how embarrassing a lot of women found this, yet she realised that Niall had managed to allay much of the girl's nervousness.

It surprised her that he had taken the time to explain as he had. She'd half expected him to be a trifle brusque with the patients but he appeared very sympathetic to their feelings.

She went to the curtain to tell him that Hannah was ready, and frowned as her gaze rested on him for a moment. He was a bit of mystery really. Her first impression had been of a man who was almost too cool, too controlled, and yet within a few short hours she'd found herself changing her views.

Underneath that icy exterior there was humour and patience and sympathy. It made her wonder which one was the real Niall Gillespie. Was it the cool professional who was determined to have things done his way? Or the man who put his patients at ease with a skill few doctors possessed? Or even the man she had glimpsed last night, a man who could laugh at himself?

She sighed, wishing she knew what the answer was because maybe then she'd know how to handle her own mixed-up feelings. If she could pop Niall Gillespie into a nice, tidy slot surely it would be easier to understand her own reaction to him?

She'd half convinced herself that this was the answer when he turned round, and suddenly she knew it would never be that simple. Niall Gillespie would never be an easy man to understand because he didn't allow people to get close enough to know him.

CHAPTER THREE

'AND last but not least we have Mrs Denning.' Sarah handed the last set of case notes to Niall Gillespie then smiled at the woman who was lying on the couch. 'How have you been, Joyce? You're looking well, I must say.'

'Blooming!' Joyce Denning laughed as she settled herself as comfortably as she could, considering the advanced state of her pregnancy. She pressed a hand to her swollen abdomen and grimaced. 'Uh-oh, here we go. Sam's off and kicking now his mum's lying down!'

'Sam?' Niall glanced up with a frowning smile as he heard what the woman said. Sarah realised that he'd only read a few lines of the case history and wondered if perhaps she should have filled him in beforehand. However, before she could say anything Joyce Denning answered his question, a faintly pensive smile on her face.

'Yes. We know he's a boy, Dr Gillespie. We were told that when the amniocentesis results came back. I think it helped make up our minds what we were going to do, especially after Sarah arranged for us to meet Robbie.'

Niall Gillespie frowned again as he quickly skimmed through the notes. Sarah saw him pause as he came to the results of the amniocentesis test, which was offered to all mothers over the age of thirty-five. The test was an invaluable aid for detecting abnormalities such as spina bifida and anencephaly, among other things. Unfortunately, it had shown that Joyce Denning's baby was suffering from Down's syndrome.

Niall put the notes down and folded his arms as he regarded the patient quietly. 'You decided to go ahead with the pregnancy even though you found out that your baby will be born with a handicap? That couldn't have been an easy decision to make, Mrs Denning.'

'No, it wasn't.' Joyce Denning laughed softly, although there was a hint of sadness in her eyes. 'It was a shock, of course. Nobody wants to hear that their child will be handicapped, do they? Ralph and I had been trying for a baby for years, you see, Dr Gillespie. We'd given up all hope of it ever happening and then, quite out of the blue, I discovered that I was pregnant at the age of forty-five!'

Sarah took Joyce's hand and squeezed it. She'd been there when the Dennings had been given the news and had seen their shock and despair. She'd also been there when they'd come back to the clinic and told Dr Henderson that they'd decided not to have the pregnancy terminated. Their courage was something which she admired enormously.

'We were quite distraught when we found out that Sam had Down's. I think we both cried for a week after we got the results. I was so shocked and upset at the time I was told that I hadn't even bothered to ask what sex the baby was. We came back to the clinic and it was Sarah who told us that the baby was a boy. It changed everything.'

'In what way?' Niall was listening with total con-
centration to what Joyce was telling him. Sarah saw
him frown as he strove to understand before he suddenly smiled. 'I see. The baby was no longer an it
but a he. Is that what you mean?'

'Yes! He was a little boy, our son. Could we
really destroy our own son just because he wasn't
perfect? I knew then what I wanted to do but it
wasn't just my decision to make. I wasn't sure if
Ralph agreed with me. Oh, I wanted to tell him how
I felt but I didn't know how to go about it. I suppose in a way I felt that I had let him down because
I wasn't giving him the perfect child we had always
longed for.'

Joyce wiped away a tear and smiled as she
looked at Sarah. 'And then Sarah arranged for us
to meet Robbie and his parents, and that was it.
Ralph and I both knew what we wanted to do.'

'And who is Robbie?' Niall glanced at Sarah and
she found herself colouring as she felt the cool
green gaze land squarely on her. She avoided his
eyes, hoping he'd attribute her heightened colour to
the fact that it was warm in the clinic that day.

'Robbie is the son of one of the midwives who
used to work here. He's a Down's syndrome child,
too. He was born a few months after I first came
here to work. Laura, his mother, had no idea that
he was going to be handicapped as there was no
reason for her to be tested. She was only twenty-
eight when she had Robbie so she didn't fall into
the ''at risk'' category. She and her husband Ian
were devastated at first and then they pulled them-

selves together and simply got on with the job of being parents.'

Sarah smiled reflectively, wondering how best to make Niall understand. 'I wish you could meet Robbie because then you'd understand. He's lively and mischievous, a real little imp, and extremely bright despite his handicap. I'm not trying to make out that there haven't been problems or that there won't be any in the future, but I know that Laura and Ian wouldn't be without him.'

'So it was Sarah, introducing you to Robbie and his parents, that helped make up your mind, then, Mrs Denning?' Niall said slowly. Sarah tried to decide what it was that she could hear in his voice but it was impossible to put a name to it. Was he surprised, or angry even? Did he think she shouldn't have interfered? She wasn't sure but she wasn't deaf to that faint nuance in his voice.

She pushed the thought aside as Joyce replied, shaking her head dismissively as the older woman praised her.

'No, it *was* what you did, Sarah. There's no doubt in my mind about that! By making us see that the future wasn't all black, we realised that we could cope with whatever was to come.' Joyce was emphatic. 'Seeing Robbie and how much joy he brings to his parents' lives, that made it easier for us to face the thought of our own child. Instead of seeing Sam as something to be ashamed of, we now think of him as special, a sort of special gift from God after all these years of waiting.'

'I think that's a wonderful attitude, Mrs Denning. Feeling like that, I'm sure you and your husband are going to enjoy this baby and not regret your decision. Now, let me take a look at you, although from the way that little fellow is kicking away there doesn't seem any cause for concern!'

They all laughed, which managed to relieve the rather emotional atmosphere. Niall gently examined Joyce, listening to the baby's heartbeat and carefully feeling his position. He stepped back as Sarah drew the sheet over Joyce and smiled.

'You're what...thirty-seven weeks now?' When Joyce nodded he continued, making notes on her chart as he did so. 'Mmm, well, Sam's head is already engaged. In other words, he's settled himself nicely right down in your pelvis ready to make his appearance in the world. You may have noticed that something felt different in the last day or so.'

'I did. I thought I was imagining it, but my "bump" did seem to be a bit lower than it had been!' Joyce said ruefully.

'No, it wasn't your imagination at all. You'll probably notice other changes as well, but I don't want you to be alarmed by them. Sam might not move about as much as he has been doing but it doesn't mean that there's anything wrong. It's simply that now his head is engaged he can't move his body about as much.

'He'll still be able to kick his legs and waggle his arms about but it won't feel as though he's playing football inside you! You may also experience some discomfort when sitting down but it's all perfectly natural at this stage. If it's any consolation it means it won't be long now.'

Niall laughed as he closed Joyce Denning's file.

'Make another appointment for next week on your way out, but I have a feeling you might not need it.'

He left the cubicle and Sarah set about helping Joyce to get down from the couch, no easy task in her advanced state of pregnancy. Joyce sighed as she slipped on her shoes. 'I hope he's right. It will be lovely to see my feet again. Why, I even went out wearing odd shoes yesterday and had no idea until someone pointed it out to me!'

Sarah laughed as she started stripping the disposable paper sheets off the couch. 'One of the trials and tribulations, I expect.'

'Too right!' Joyce picked up her bag then glanced towards the corridor where Niall Gillespie was just disappearing from sight. 'I like the new man, Sarah. He's a real sweetie, isn't he? Don't get me wrong, Dr Henderson was lovely but Dr Gillespie makes you feel so...well, so special, I guess. I think it's because he really concentrates on what you're telling him, and doesn't look as though he's got a million other things more important to attend to. Is he married, do you know?'

Sarah shrugged, although she couldn't deny that her heart seemed to skip a beat at the thought. 'I've no idea. Nobody seems to know much about his private life.'

'Hmm. I'd have said he would be, a lovely man like that, and yet there's something rather lonely about him which makes me wonder.' Joyce laughed self-consciously. 'Listen to me! Must be the hormones running riot again. I don't suppose Dr Gillespie would appreciate us discussing him like this. Nice as he is, I get the feeling that he likes to keep himself to himself, don't you?'

Joyce Denning gave Sarah a little wave as she left. Sarah set about tidying the examination room, trying not to dwell too much on what Joyce had said. Yet the words seemed to be stuck in her mind like a needle in the groove of a record.

Was Niall Gillespie married?

Suddenly impatient with herself, she bundled up the sheets, took them to the disposal shute then went to wash her hands. Surely she had better things to worry about than Niall Gillespie's marital status! she chided herself. But as she turned off the tap she caught a glimpse of herself in the tiny mirror above the basin and frowned as she saw the curiosity that still shadowed her hazel eyes.

She sighed in defeat, realising that she was kidding herself if she tried to pretend she wasn't interested in him. Whether she liked the idea or not, Niall Gillespie intrigued her. He was like an enigma hidden inside a puzzle, and there were so many layers wrapped around him that unwrapping them might prove an impossible task—but she knew with sudden certainty that was what she wanted to do.

She wanted to peel away the layers, solve the puzzles, break the enigma's code…and get to the real heart of the man beneath!

'Sarah, can you get down to the main doors right away? We have problems!'

Irene didn't waste any more time on explanations as she put down the phone. Sarah left the rest of her lunch on the staffroom table as she headed for the door. She couldn't begin to imagine what was wrong but if Irene thought it necessary to call her then it was something serious.

There was quite a crowd gathered by the big glass doors. Sarah pushed her way through the group of people, wondering who on earth they all were. Irene was kneeling on the floor next to a young girl of about eighteen, who was sprawled on the tiles. It was obvious that she was heavily pregnant and barely conscious from the look of her.

'What happened? Who is she? And who are all this lot?' Sarah shot a stream of questions at Irene as she dropped down beside her.

'Her name's Ariel. That's all I've been able to get out of anyone so far.' Irene grimaced as she glanced up at the crowd. 'They're part of that band of New Age travellers who are camped just outside town.'

'I see.' Sarah nodded, realising at once why they all looked so dirty and tattered. There had been a lot of grumbling in the town at first when they'd set up camp a month or so earlier, but it had gradually died down when the travellers hadn't caused any problems.

'How is she? Is she going to be all right?'

Sarah glanced at the anxious face of the young man who was bending over them. 'Can you tell us what happened and how…Ariel came to be in this state?'

'I don't know! She seemed fine up till yesterday…' The young man swallowed as he ran a grimy hand over his eyes. 'She started complaining of a headache yesterday afternoon, said she could see lots of flashing lights, stuff like that.' He shrugged. 'I didn't think much of it at first and then she was sick all night long. Couldn't seem to keep anything down her. This morning she started saying that she had pains in her stomach so we decided to bring her here. She passed out just as we were getting her out of the van.'

Sarah glanced out of the doors to where a battered purple truck was parked then turned her attention back to the young girl. Lifting up various dingy layers of clothing, she quickly examined the girl's ankles and lower legs, trying to hide her dismay when she saw how swollen they were. Her skin was so distended with fluid that when Sarah gently pressed it her fingertips left small indentations behind.

'Have you seen how swollen her legs are, Irene?' she asked quietly, drawing the other woman's attention to what she had discovered.

'Yes. I spotted that right away. That's why I called you. Add that to everything else, Sarah, and what do we have?' Irene said grimly.

'Eclampsia?' Sarah frowned. 'In this day and age? It's usually detected well before this stage…' She paused. 'That is, assuming that the mother has proper antenatal care. And that seems unlikely in this case.'

'Unfortunately, I think you're right.' Irene got to her feet and hurried over to the phone to summon assistance. Within minutes a porter appeared with a trolley and between them they managed to lift Ariel onto it. She was moaning softly now, although it was obvious that she had no real idea where she was.

'Wait! Where are you taking her?' The young man tried to stop them as they started to push the trolley towards the lift. Sarah nodded to Irene to carry on, neatly forestalling him as he went to follow them.

'I'm sorry but you can't go with her. Ariel is very, very sick and if we don't treat her right away she could die. As it is, it will be touch and go if the baby survives.'

Sarah knew she was being unusually harsh in laying down the facts yet she sensed that it was the only way to prevent an ugly confrontation. She glanced at the other travellers who were gathered in the foyer, wondering if she should summon assistance. However, they appeared more shocked than anything else, and Sarah quickly realised just how young most of them were, barely out of their teens.

'Wh-what's wrong with her?'

There was a lot less defiance in the young man's voice now and Sarah's tone softened. 'From what we can tell, Ariel might be suffering from eclampsia, although it will be up to the doctor to decide that.'

'What is it, this ec-eclam—?'

'Eclampsia,' Sarah repeated. 'It starts when a pregnant woman's blood pressure rises and the level of uric acid in her blood increases. She then begins retaining fluid. This is a sort of early-warning stage called pre-eclampsia. However, if it isn't treated the next stage is when the woman starts excreting protein in her urine.

'If the condition is allowed to go untreated, the danger is that the placenta will fail to work properly as clots and fatty acids build up in the arteries. Then the baby will be born prematurely. However, the biggest worry of all is that pre-eclampsia will progress to eclampsia, which is very dangerous for both the mother and child. Unfortunately, the symptoms you described are indicative of that.

'It rarely reaches this stage nowadays as it's usually detected early on during routine antenatal checks. But I don't imagine that Ariel has been attending a clinic, has she?'

He shook his head. 'No. Ariel said that having a baby isn't like being ill or anything. She didn't want to be messed around by any doctors.'

Sarah sighed. 'Unfortunately, things can and do go wrong. Now we can only hope that we can repair some of the damage which has been done through lack of proper medical care.'

'Can…can I stay with her?' The young man shuffled his feet. 'The baby's mine, you see.'

'Well, yes, I suppose so. You won't be able to actually stay with her but you can go to the relatives' room and wait there. However, I'm afraid the rest of you will have to leave.'

There was a lot of grumbling but eventually the rest of the group left. Sarah led the way along the corridor to the waiting-room. 'You can wait in here. There's coffee in the machine along the hall. Have you got some change?'

'Yes…thanks. Will you tell Ariel that I'm here? It might help her.'

'Of course. What's your name?' Sarah asked, wishing it were that easy. Although *pre*-eclampsia was relatively common, affecting between five and ten per cent of all pregnant women, she'd seen only one case of eclampsia before. She'd been in training then and would never forget that poor woman. She, too, had refused antenatal care and it had cost her her life.

'Jason.'

'All right, then, Jason. I'll come back and let you know how she is as soon as I can.' Sarah hurried away, leaving the young man hunched up in a chair, looking miserable. She took the lift, sending up a little prayer that it wasn't too late for either Ariel or her baby.

'Blood pressure one-forty over ninety-five, Doctor.' Sarah made a note on the chart then slid it into the pocket at the foot of the bed.

'Right, we need to get that down. And get something into her to prevent her convulsing.' Niall's tone was grim as he finished his examination. 'When did her boyfriend say this all started?'

'Yesterday afternoon,' Sarah replied quietly.

'Hell and damnation! And they didn't think to do something about it until now!' He made no attempt to disguise his anger as he turned to glare at her, as though she were the one responsible for Ariel's condition.

She met his gaze levelly, understanding that it was frustration that caused him to be so annoyed.

This sort of thing simply shouldn't happen in this day and age.

'I doubt if either of them realised that it was so serious,' she said softly.

'I know.' Niall sighed. 'Sorry. It's just so damn frustrating!'

He gave her a rueful smile then turned back to Irene, who was monitoring the condition of Ariel's baby. Sarah moved away to get the intravenous drip that would be needed, trying to stop her heart from jumping up and down. Niall's smile was alarmingly potent and did little for her peace of mind!

'I'm not happy with what I'm getting, Dr Gillespie.' Irene frowned as she scanned the print-out from the foetal monitor. 'The baby's heart seems to be slowing down.'

'Let me see.' Niall quickly scanned the strip of tape. 'I see what you mean. I'm not happy with that at all. I think we need to—'

He stopped abruptly as Ariel gave a moaning gasp then suddenly went rigid. 'Right, everyone, she's convulsing. Let's get things moving. Sarah, get that line into her immediately. We'll give her thiopentone sodium for the seizures. Then we'll need to do a section if we're to have any hope of saving this baby.'

Everyone set to work at once, each going about the task of saving Ariel and her child. Sarah set up the intravenous drip, her heart going out to the girl as she lay there, oblivious to what was happening. After a few moments Ariel relaxed, her breathing slowing as she lapsed into unconsciousness. Sarah prayed that the drugs would prevent her having a second convulsion but there were no guarantees at this stage.

'We'll need to be extra careful about infection.' Niall frowned as he saw how dirty Ariel's legs were. 'God knows how she got into this state.'

'There's a group of New Age travellers camped just outside town. She's with them,' Sarah explained as she carefully washed the girls abdomen with antiseptic solution.

'That's no excuse. I've worked in countries where water is more precious than gold and yet the people still keep themselves clean!' Niall's tone was biting, the anger Sarah had sensed before once more in evidence.

She shot him a quick glance, wondering what the cause of it really was. It seemed to stem from something deeper than just a concern for Ariel's welfare. It was as though…as though the danger their patient and her unborn child were in affected him personally.

Sarah frowned as she carried on with what she was doing, making a thorough job of ensuring that at least the site of the incision would be free from germs. She'd thought before that Niall was a mystery but she was only just beginning to realise how right she'd been.

What had made Niall Gillespie into the man he was today? She wished with all her heart that she knew, even though she couldn't understand why it should be so important to her.

CHAPTER FOUR

'GET her along to the special care unit immediately, Irene. She'll need monitoring closely for the next twenty-four hours—if she survives that long.' Niall sighed heavily as he looked at the tiny scrap lying in the incubator. 'It's going to be touch and go, poor little mite.'

Irene smiled sadly. 'Not much of a start to life, is it? She barely weighs three pounds and her breathing isn't good.'

'Normally she would have had a better chance if she could have gone to term but in this case there was no question of leaving her.' Niall shrugged. 'As it is, she's lucky to be alive so let's try to be positive. She's got a far better chance than she had an hour ago.'

Sarah sighed as she ran a gentle finger down the baby's scrawny little arm. The child's skin was tinged red where the blood vessels were showing through because of her lack of body fat. Ariel's pre-eclampsia had meant that the placenta hadn't been working as well as it should have been so that the baby had been undernourished in the womb.

She was breathing rapidly, making tiny grunting noises as she struggled for air. Because she was several weeks premature, her lungs didn't contain sufficient surfactant to help them expand, which meant that the baby had to work even harder to breathe and could soon become exhausted.

She would be given oxygen in the special care unit to avoid that happening, probably via a tiny catheter in her nostril. Blood samples would also be taken at regular intervals to test the amount of oxygen in her blood, but it was going to be touch and go, as Niall had said. Sarah sent up a silent prayer that the poor little mite would make it.

'Right, let's get finished up here.' Niall set to the task of dealing with the baby's mother as Irene briskly wheeled the crib from the room. Ariel had already been given an injection of oxytocin to make the placenta peel away from the wall of the uterus. Now it was just a question of removing it and closing the incision.

He worked swiftly and deftly as he stitched the cut in the uterus layer by layer with absorbable sutures. Sarah helped him, carefully suctioning out any blood and amniotic fluid before the abdominal wall itself was repaired. The non-absorbable sutures used for this purpose would need to be removed at a later date.

It all took some time but Sarah felt privileged to be helping. She'd seen many Caesarean sections performed but she'd rarely seen one done with the degree of skill and care which Niall Gillespie had shown. She checked the instruments and swabs then placed everything on the trolley and moved it away, smiling at Helen who had been drafted in to help and had just witnessed her very first Caesarean section.

'He's brilliant, isn't he?' There was a touch of

hero-worship in the look Helen cast towards the bed, where Niall was checking Ariel's pulse. Ariel was still deeply unconscious, thanks to the intravenous drip, and mercifully had shown no further signs of any seizures.

Sarah glanced back and felt her heart give that strange little leap it had learned to do in the past few days. She frowned as her eyes lingered on Niall's lowered head, wondering what it was about this man and no other that made her react this way...

'Sarah?'

Helen prompted her when she failed to answer and hastily she dragged her thoughts back into line. 'Yes, he is good. Dr Henderson was highly skilled but Niall is a real expert.'

'Niall?' Helen teased. 'Mmm, so we're at the first-name stage, are we? So much for "he just dropped me off"! I wonder what really happened last night?'

Sarah blushed furiously, wondering when she had started thinking about him as 'Niall.' It had never crossed her mind to call Dr Henderson by anything other than his full title, yet here she was making free with this man's name as though they were...intimately acquainted!

The thought, especially the last two words of it, were enough to make her blush even harder, and she heard Helen giggle as she put her own interpretation on the reason for Sarah's heightened colour.

'You, Sarah Harris, are a dark horse! Wait till I tell everyone that you've been holding out on us.'

'I haven't. I mean—'

She got no further as Niall beckoned to her. She schooled her features into a purely professional smile as she went over to him but she could do nothing about her pink cheeks. She saw his eyes linger on her flushed face for a moment before he looked back at the girl on the bed.

'She seems to be holding her own. Her blood pressure has come down and it doesn't appear that she's going to have another convulsion, although, of course, we can't be sure of that at this stage. I want her put in a side room and kept very quiet. We'll keep her on the thiopentone sodium and see how she goes. But she's to have no visitors and no stimulation of any kind until we're certain the danger period is past.'

His tone was suddenly very grave. 'There's still the chance that things could go wrong so let's be prepared for it. I want her specialled for the next forty-eight hours at least, and possibly for longer.'

Sarah frowned. 'I'm not sure we have the staff for that. We've had so many budget cuts that staffing levels have been cut to the bone.'

'Then we'll just have to do something about it!' he said grimly as he moved away from the bed. He headed briskly for the door then paused to glance back. 'Thank you, Sarah. You did an excellent job today. I appreciate your professionalism.'

He was gone before Sarah could say anything, the door swinging back and forth on its hinges with the abruptness of his departure. She took a small breath but it didn't negate the pleasure she felt at his praise. Niall Gillespie was such a professional himself that for him to have said that about her work meant a lot to her...

She quickly edited the next thought, not wanting to dwell on it. If it wasn't only her professionalism that she wanted him to recognise then that was by the by. Allowing herself to indulge in silly fantasies where Niall found other things to appreciate about her, that was simply opening herself up to a whole load of heartache!

'But why can't I see her? I want to know she's all right!'

Sarah sighed as she saw the other people in the waiting-room exchange uneasy glances. She beckoned Jason to follow her along the corridor, out of earshot of the other relatives who were waiting for news.

'Ariel is still very, very ill. At the moment she's under sedation and wouldn't even know you were there. Unfortunately, she had a convulsion and the last thing we want is for her to have any more,' she explained quietly but firmly. 'That's why Dr Gillespie has given strict instructions that she isn't to have any visitors at present.'

'A convulsion?' Jason repeated, sounding stunned. 'You mean some sort of...of fit?'

'Yes. It was the result of the eclampsia. Once Ariel wakes up she'll still need to be on an intravenous drip for a while to prevent any further convulsions. But any undue excitement could cause a relapse in her condition and that is what we're trying to avoid.'

'I see. But what about the baby? Is...is it all

right?' He swallowed hard, obviously upset by what he had been told. Sarah sympathised with him because it was a lot to take in. However, the welfare of the mother and child were her most pressing concern.

'She's in the special care unit. Dr Gillespie had to deliver her by Caesarean section or she wouldn't have survived. She's very small, barely three pounds, and she's having trouble breathing, which is quite common with babies who are premature. The next few hours will be crucial for her as well.'

'She? It's a little girl?' Tears ran unashamedly down Jason's face now. 'Ariel said it would be a girl. She wanted to call her Star.'

Sarah touched his arm, wishing that she could offer more in the way of reassurance. However, it wouldn't be fair to build up his hopes by playing down how ill the baby was. 'That's a beautiful name. I'll make sure that the nurses in the special care unit put it on her cot.'

'Thanks. Can I see her, do you think?' Jason wiped his nose on his sleeve and managed a smile. Sarah realised that under the grime he was a nice-looking boy. 'Oh, I know I can't hold her or anything, but if I could just see her then I can tell Ariel what she looks like. Ariel will want to know as soon as she wakes up.'

'Well...' Sarah sighed as she glanced at his clothes. 'Look, Jason, there isn't an easy way to say this so I may as well come straight out with it—there's no way that you can go anywhere near the special care unit in that state. The babies in there are very vulnerable to infection and you could be carrying all sorts of germs on you.'

He flushed as he looked down at himself. 'Oh. I see. But what if I got cleaned up—then could I see her?' he asked hopefully.

'Of course you can. Is there anywhere you can go to have a bath and get a change of clothes?' she said encouragingly.

'Well, no.' He shook his head, his face mirroring his disappointment. 'There's a stream near where we're camped but that's it. And as for clothes... well, these are all I've got.'

Sarah bit her lip, wondering if there was a solution. Despite his ragged state, it was obvious that Jason cared deeply about Ariel and the baby. She frowned as an idea surfaced, wondering what he would think of it.

'There is someone who might be willing to help. You're camped quite close to the church, aren't you? What if I give the vicar a ring to see if he can help out?' she suggested quietly. 'He's a really nice man and he's usually more than happy to do all he can.'

'I don't know...' Jason was obviously dubious. 'I can't see him wanting to help the likes of me. Most folk don't want to when we're involved,' he added bitterly.

'Maybe they're put off by the way you look.' Sarah looked pointedly at the matted dreadlocks he was sporting down the centre of his head. Both sides of his head had been shaved and adorned with tattoos, the silver studs which peppered his ears providing the finishing touches.

Jason's appearance was enough to make most people wary, and she felt a momentary qualm as she thought about what she'd suggested. However, when he nodded his agreement she was left with little choice but to see what could be arranged.

She went to the office and put through the call, hesitantly explaining to the vicar why she was ringing. She'd met him several times when he'd been into the maternity unit to visit parishioners, and had always found him a down-to-earth sort of man. Now she smiled in relief as he immediately offered assistance, brushing aside her warnings about Jason's appearance with a rueful laugh.

As he succinctly explained, he had been vicar of an inner-city parish, before moving to Dalverston, and had done a lot of work there with the homeless. He had learned very early on not to be put off by appearances!

Jason was touchingly grateful when she went back and told him what had been arranged. He thanked her profusely then hurried off to the vicarage. Sarah watched him go with a smile on her face as she realised that the vicar had been right. Appearances counted for very little. It was what was underneath that mattered, what a person was really like beneath the outward trappings. That brought her thoughts right back to Niall Gillespie again. Not that they ever seemed to be very far away from him!

'Pick you up at seven, OK?'

'Well, I don't know…' Sarah bit back a sigh as she saw Mike's face drop as he anticipated her refusal. She fixed a smile to her mouth, trying to ignore her aching feet and back. 'Sure. I'll see you later, then.'

'Great!' Mike beamed as he shot off down the drive, the noisy splutter of his motorbike sending a flock of birds winging from the trees. Sarah followed more slowly, wishing she'd had the courage to take the bull by the horns and tell Mike that she didn't want to see the film with him tonight.

She hated to disappoint him and yet she was going to have to do so very soon. It would be far kinder to break off with Mike sooner rather than later, before he started to believe that things were more serious than they were.

She was so lost in her thoughts that she didn't notice the car that was coming down the drive behind her. It was only as it came level with her that she glanced round and felt her heart leap as she recognised Niall Gillespie behind the wheel.

He drew to a halt alongside her and wound down the window. 'Do you want a lift? I'm going your way.'

'Oh, I... Well...' She was so nonplussed by the offer that she didn't know what to say. Someone sounded their hooter and Niall glanced round impatiently.

'Come on, hop in. I seem to be holding up traffic.'

She had no recourse but to do as he'd suggested. She opened the car door and slid into the seat, half expecting Niall to drive off immediately, but he waited until she had fastened her seat belt securely before making any attempt to move.

He turned the car out of the gates, keeping his speed down as they made their way through the rush-hour traffic. He drove calmly and competently, his every move unhurried as he wove through the busy streets.

Sarah found herself relaxing, secure in the knowledge that she was in safe hands. She'd never felt like that on the few occasions she'd agreed to travel on the back of Mike's motorbike, she thought wryly. Then she'd been so on edge that she'd found herself barely able to breathe!

'Penny for them?'

She started, giving an embarrassed laugh as she realised she'd been daydreaming. 'Sorry, I was miles away.' She looked round, not wanting to go into detail about what she'd been thinking. 'Are you sure this isn't taking you out of your way?'

'Not at all. I live down by the river, the old Jackson house. Do you know it?' he replied smoothly.

'I'm not sure... It isn't that run-down old farm-house at the bottom of Pepper Lane, is it?' she asked incredulously.

'That's the one!' Niall laughed at her astonishment. 'I expect you think I'm mad, taking on a place like that.'

'Well...' She wasn't sure what to answer.

'Mmm, I see that tact is another of your virtues.' Niall smiled as he turned the car off the main road and headed out of the centre of town.

'Another?' she queried before she could stop herself, then coloured as she realised how it had sounded. 'Forget I said that. I'm not fishing for compliments!'

'You wouldn't need to fish too hard, Sarah,' he said quietly. 'I meant what I said this afternoon about appreciating your professionalism. And it's obvious to anyone that not only are you highly skilled at your job but that you care a great deal about your patients. That is rare enough these days. Too often medicine is seen as a career rather than a vocation.'

She looked away, afraid that her expression might betray how much she appreciated the compliment. It meant a lot to her that he should think that, more than it would have meant if anyone else had said the same thing.

'I love this job,' she said quickly, not completely comfortable with that thought. 'I always wanted to be a nurse right from when I was small, but it was only when I did a stint on the maternity wing while I was a student that I realised I wanted to specialise in midwifery. There's something magical about each birth and being there at the beginning of a new life.'

She gave an embarrassed laugh. 'I don't suppose I need to tell you that, do I? Why else did you decide to go into obstetrics?'

Niall's hands tightened on the steering-wheel so that his knuckles gleamed whitely through his skin. 'My reasons weren't quite the same as yours, Sarah.'

He didn't add anything more, leaving a small silence which was suddenly full of questions. What had he meant by that? she wondered. Niall had sounded almost…tortured as he'd made that statement, but she had no idea why.

She bit her lip in a quandary of indecision, longing to ask him to explain but afraid to do so because she sensed it was something he didn't want to talk about. It was yet another mystery to add to all the others surrounding this man. At every turn it seemed that instead of finding out more about him she knew even less. It was deeply frustrating!

In an effort to distract herself from the problem, Sarah returned the conversation to what they'd been talking about a few minutes earlier. 'What made you decide to buy the old Jackson house anyway? Surely you could have found some place in a lot better condition?'

'I could, but none of the properties on the market had what I wanted most, i.e. land.' He cast her a quick glance and she had the oddest feeling that he was trying to look deep inside her mind. It unsettled her to wonder what he might find there, considering all the confusion she felt at present.

She looked down at her hands, pleating a fold of her uniform dress with fingers which were just a bit unsteady. 'You're a keen gardener, then? Is that why you wanted land?' She paused, struck by a strangely unpalatable thought. 'Or do you have a family and wanted them to have some place to play?'

'No. I don't have children, or a wife.' His voice grated, sending a shiver through her whole body. She shot him a quick look from beneath lowered lashes but his face gave nothing away.

He took a deep breath, making an obvious effort

to lighten the sombre mood. 'However, I do have a very demanding female in my life. She's the reason I wanted plenty of space.' He turned and smiled at her, his eyes crinkling at the corners as he saw her mouth form a silent 'Oh' of surprise. 'Would you like to meet her, Sarah? I think you and she would get on very well, and that's a *real* compliment because this lady of mine doesn't take kindly to other females.'

He gave a gently mocking laugh, although Sarah had no idea what the joke was. She took a quick breath, wondering how she could refuse the offer without letting him know why she was doing so. The thought of meeting this special woman in Niall's life wasn't one she relished, in all truth! Yet as she looked into his laughing green eyes and felt her heart perform its customary somersault, she knew she wasn't going to refuse.

She was too curious to turn down the chance of learning something about him...even though she wasn't going to like it!

'And here she is. Her name is Adair. So what do you think, Sarah? Is she as beautiful as you expected her to be?'

Sarah knew that Niall was teasing her but she simply couldn't rise to the occasion. She took a gulping breath as he held out his arm. His hand and forearm were encased in a heavy leather gauntlet, but, then, it would need some sort of protection against the wicked-looking talons of the huge red-coloured bird that was perched on it!

'She's beautiful...' Sarah struggled to control the

rush of emotions she felt, but she wasn't sure her voice didn't betray a little too much of her feelings. 'What sort of bird is she?'

'A red buzzard. Or, if you prefer her official title, *Accipitridae buteo buteo*.' He ran his hand gently over the bird's proud head, smiling as she made soft little cries in response. 'I've had her three years and she's the reason I needed so much land.'

He turned to look round the huge cage in which the bird lived. 'Adair needs a lot of space. This flight is thirty-five feet long and half that again in both height and width. It means that she can exercise her wings even when I don't have time to let her fly free.'

'Why did you call her Adair?' Sarah asked softly, lowering her voice to match his quiet tone, although the bird's head instantly swivelled in her direction, its yellow-ringed eyes fixing Sarah with an unblinking stare.

'After the American firefighter, Red Adair. It suited both her colouring and the way I came to get her.'

'That sounds very intriguing.' Sarah smiled. 'You can't leave it at that, Niall, you have to tell me the whole story!'

He laughed. 'Of course, if you're interested.' He carried on when she nodded.

'An oil tanker ran out of control and crashed one day close to the hospital where I used to work. It set a large area of woodland alight, trapping several people who were camping there at the time. All available staff were drafted in to deal with the emergency and I was asked to go to the site to attend to one of the casualties, a woman who'd been hit by a falling tree. She was seven months pregnant and had gone into labour with the shock.'

'It must have been like a nightmare.' Sarah shivered, picturing the scene. 'What happened? Did the baby survive?'

Niall shook his head sadly. 'No. I couldn't do anything for it. It was stillborn. The best I could do was ensure that the mother survived. Everyone was upset, as you can imagine—the firefighters, the paramedics, the police—but there wasn't anything anyone could have done. Anyway, as we were preparing to leave, I noticed something lying on the ground. It was a bird, only a fledgling really. Maybe it had been flying overhead when the tanker blew up and the blast knocked it out—I'm not sure. It was still alive so I took it home with me.' He shrugged. 'I just couldn't bear the thought of leaving it there to die.'

'And that fledgling was Adair. You called her that because she'd survived an oil fire, like the real Red Adair who puts out fires in oil wells all around the world?' Sarah laughed softly, touched by the story and the fact that Niall should have cared about the plight of this beautiful creature.

'That's right. It seemed appropriate.' He smiled as he stroked the bird's head once again. 'I didn't think she'd make it at first because of the shock. But she came through in the end. I had to hand-rear her, of course, which meant that I couldn't return her to the wild as she wouldn't have survived. So I kept her and fly her whenever possible. She seems happy enough.'

'She does. And very proprietorial.' Sarah laughed as Adair gave her another sly sideways look. 'I think she feels quite possessive about you!'

'I know. But, then, she's never had to share me with anyone, so it's understandable.' He set the bird back on its perch then stripped off the heavy leather glove so that he could open the inner door of the cage.

Sarah followed him into the entryway, waiting while he locked the inner door before opening the outside gate. She cast a swift glance back, watching as Adair flew gracefully down the length of the cage to land on the branch of a tree which had been cleverly incorporated into it to provide a natural perch for her.

What had Niall meant when he'd said that Adair had never had to share him? That there was no woman in his life and that there hadn't been one for the past three years?

It seemed inconceivable. Niall Gillespie was an extremely attractive man and many women would have been keen to provide him with company, and a whole lot more! Yet Sarah sensed that it was true. The idea stunned her.

Why had he avoided any relationships in the past few years? she wondered. Was it just that he'd chosen to concentrate on his career to the exclusion of everything else? Or was there another reason?

She frowned as she tried to work out the answer while she followed him back to the car. It was obvious that Niall was caught up in the demands of his profession so she could understand why he'd had little time for anything else. Yet she sensed there was another reason for the life he had chosen.

Had Niall been deeply hurt in the past by a relationship that had gone wrong? Was that why he had fought shy of any further involvements and concentrated solely on his work?

She suspected that was the real answer and felt a sudden pang of regret. Niall Gillespie must have loved the woman who had let him down very much for it to have caused such lasting damage. It could take years before he was ready to commit himself to another relationship, if indeed he was ever able to do so. The plain truth was that he might never want to risk falling in love again.

Sarah got back into the car, wondering why that thought should leave her feeling so empty.

CHAPTER FIVE

'SO HOW did the date go? Did you have a good time?'

'Date?' Sarah repeated blankly.

'Your trip to the cinema with Mike. Don't tell me you've forgotten about it already.' Irene laughed as she picked up a plastic apron. 'Or could it be that you have someone else on your mind—like our handsome Niall, for instance?'

'Of course not! Don't be ridiculous. I just didn't understand what you meant, that's all!' Sarah bit her lip as she saw the look Irene gave her, wishing she hadn't been quite so vehement in denying the teasing accusation. It was just that there'd been more than a grain of truth in what Irene had said and it stung to realise it.

She sighed as she collected an apron from the pile, ruefully acknowledging that she hardly remembered a thing about her evening out with Mike Dawson. If anyone had asked, she couldn't even have told them which film they'd seen. For the past two days Niall Gillespie had occupied her thoughts from the moment she'd got up in the morning to the time she'd gone to bed at night!

Deciding that it was better to let the matter drop, Sarah didn't say anything more as she followed Irene to the delivery room. However, it wasn't that easy to rid her mind of the jumble of conflicting thoughts.

It had been two days since Niall had driven her home that second time and introduced her to Adair. Sarah hadn't told anyone about that and had no intention of doing so, especially not after what Irene had said just now!

She'd been off duty since then and had spent the time catching up on housework in the small terraced cottage she rented. In a way she'd been glad of the breathing space because that visit to Niall's house had left her feeling more unsettled than ever. She'd come to the conclusion late last night that it would be better to keep well away from him for a while, and the coming week seemed like the perfect opportunity.

She was working nights for the next five days so there would be little chance of running into him. It would give her time to get her life back on track and stop thinking about him all the time, or that was what she had told herself, anyway. Now she realised that it wasn't going to be that easy to put Niall out of her mind.

'Right, I don't think we're going to have any major problems other than the fact that Trisha is going to be a pain. She's done nothing but complain since she was brought in.' Irene paused outside the delivery room and rolled her eyes. 'She's demanding an epidural but let's see if we can talk her out of it. Although I don't hold out too much hope!'

Sarah laughed as she followed Irene into the room, making a determined effort to keep her mind on her job. The young woman who was lying on the bed looked round and her mouth pursed with annoyance as soon as she saw them.

'I said that I wanted an injection! Why haven't I been given one?'

'I've paged Dr Patel to come and take a look at you, Trisha,' Irene said calmly. 'She'll call the anaesthetist down to give you the injection if you decide it's what you really want.'

'Of course it's what I want! What's the point of being in agony when there's no need?' Trisha retorted, glaring at them.

Sarah moved to the bed to check how far Trisha's cervix had dilated. It was barely three centimetres as yet, showing that labour was only in its early stages and that the contractions should be quite short and far apart. It could be some time before her cervix dilated to the ten centimetres necessary to allow the baby to be born.

She checked the foetal monitor as well, pleased to see that the baby was obviously a lot calmer than its irate mother. 'Everything is coming along really well, Trisha,' she soothed. 'Obviously, if you feel you want an epidural that much then I'm sure Dr Patel will agree. However, you do understand that once your body is numb from the waist down you won't be able to feel the contractions, don't you?'

Trisha gave her a cold-eyed stare. 'Of course I understand. I'm not stupid. That's why I want it! It's bad enough having this kid without having to suffer all this agony as well—' She broke off and screamed. 'Oh-h…do something, can't you? That's what you're here for!'

Irene raised her eyebrows at Sarah. 'I'll give Meena another call. OK?'

Sarah nodded as she set about calming Trisha down, no easy task in view of the fact that the young woman was determined to make things as difficult as possible for everyone. Each contraction was met by a scream so that it was a relief when Meena Patel arrived and immediately agreed that the anaesthetist should be summoned.

Sarah made the call although, like Irene, she had conflicting views on the benefits of epidural anaesthesia. While it meant that a woman didn't experience any pain, it also meant that she could feel nothing in the lower part of her body, making it far more difficult for her to work with her contractions. However, in a case like this, where the mother refused to consider any other options, there was little anyone could do but go along with her wishes.

Administering the anaesthetic, it was like a nightmare. It took both Sarah and Irene to keep Trisha still so that the injection could be given safely into the space between the spinal cord and the dura, the membrane which surrounded it. It was often uncomfortable for a woman in labour to lie on her side while the anaesthetic was administered but most coped with the discomfort. However, Trisha was vociferous as she let them know her views, almost turning the air blue with her curses.

Geoff Redway, the anaesthetist, breathed a sigh of relief once it was over, his expression saying everything he couldn't put into words in front of the patient. Sarah laughed as she saw him out into the corridor where he offered his sympathies for what she had to put up with!

She gave him a wave as he headed for the lift and sanity, as he succinctly put it. However, her smile faded abruptly as the lift doors opened just then and Niall stepped out. There was a moment when their eyes met which couldn't have lasted longer than a second and yet she felt as though a whole lifetime could have been lived in that time.

Her eyes seemed to be locked to Niall's, held there by some force beyond her control so that when he suddenly turned and walked swiftly in the opposite direction she felt a searing sense of anti-climax.

She took a small breath, unaware until that moment that she had stopped breathing. Every nerve in her body seemed to be thrumming with tension, a feeling of heat invading each cell. It took her all her time to make her way back into the room, her movements jerkily uncoordinated so that the door slipped from her hand and slammed shut.

'You all right, Sarah?'

Irene's concerned voice was the stimulus she needed to break the spell. She managed a ragged smile but she knew what it cost her to act normally when nothing felt normal any longer.

'I'm fine, thanks. Or as fine as I'm going to be for the next few hours!' she added, glancing pointedly at Trisha.

Irene laughed, as she'd been meant to, turning her attention back to their patient now that she was sure nothing was wrong. Sarah went to assist her, wishing with all her heart *she* were as certain of that.

Something *was* wrong. Something odd was happening to her. It had started the first time she'd seen Niall Gillespie, and day by day it seemed to be getting worse!

'It's a boy, Trisha. A lovely little boy. Do you want to hold him?' Sarah finished tying the baby's cord and offered him to the young woman.

'Ugh, no! Look at him. He's all sticky and gungy…' Trisha closed her eyes as though just the sight of her baby son disgusted her.

Sarah had a sudden urge to shake her but she controlled it. Childbirth affected every woman differently and it was wrong to judge Trisha when she was obviously overwrought. It might have helped if there had been someone with her throughout her labour but there had been no sign of anyone since she'd been brought in by ambulance. It made Sarah wonder where the baby's father was, or even if he was still around. Maybe that explained Trisha's attitude towards the child?

Sighing at the thought, she carried the baby over to the table and ran through all the usual checks, noting down his weight and length, how big his head was. He regarded her solemnly with that look some new babies had, as though they had been through this all before and were weary of the fuss.

Sarah smiled as she spoke to him softly, watching how his eyes struggled to focus on her face. She had a warm bath all ready to wash him and she laughed as she saw his face pucker when she gently lowered him into the water, as though he wasn't too sure about this new experience.

'Come on, sweetheart,' she soothed softly. 'You know you like this. It's just like being back in Mummy's tummy.'

'Probably better,' Irene put in wryly from behind her. 'Imagine being stuck inside there for nine months!'

'Now, now, is that any way to speak about our new mum?' Sarah said reprovingly, trying not to laugh.

'No, but it's true.' Irene sighed. 'I'm getting too old for this. There were a couple of times when I felt like slapping that young madam. Especially when you see what a beautiful little boy she's got. Some women would give their right arms for a perfect child like this.' She lowered her voice to a whisper. 'Joyce Denning has just had her baby. Dr Gillespie came in specially to be at the birth.'

'They're all right, both Joyce and Sam, I mean?' Sarah asked just as quietly.

'Fine. From what I just heard in the staffroom, it wasn't an easy labour but, you know Joyce, she just got on with it. She and her husband asked if they could have some time alone with Sam before he's taken away for all the tests.'

'And Nia—Dr Gillespie agreed?' Sarah quickly corrected herself, trying not to notice the old-fashioned look Irene gave her.

'Yes. Why? You sound surprised.'

Sarah shrugged. 'Oh, nothing. It's just that the first day he was here he told me off about not doing things by the book. You know, weighing and measuring and so on before letting the mother hold the baby. I'm just surprised that he agreed to Joyce's request, I suppose.'

Irene laughed. 'Knowing you, I imagine you left him in little doubt of your views on the matter, Sarah! Maybe you talked him round to your way of thinking, eh?'

Irene moved away as Trisha called plaintively from the bed, demanding a drink of water. Sarah finished bathing the baby, trying to ignore the warm little glow in her heart at the thought that Niall might have taken account of her views...

She sighed as she carefully dried the little boy with a warm towel, then set about tagging his wrist and ankle with identity bands. Who was she kidding? If Niall had decided to do things differently in this instance it had been out of deference to Joyce's wishes. It had had nothing to do with her, Sarah Harris!

'He's just beautiful, Joyce.'

Sarah ran the tip of her finger down Sam's soft cheek. He responded by turning his head towards her, his eyes screwed up as he greedily searched for food.

'Mmm, he knows what he wants, doesn't he?' Joyce laughed as she lifted him out of his cot and brushed a kiss over the top of his blond head. His handicap was clear to see in the slanting, widely spaced eyes and flattened features, but Sarah knew that Joyce had come to terms with that during her pregnancy.

Joyce had been far more concerned about Sam's

general health as Down's babies could suffer from a variety of problems, including heart defects and intestinal malformations. Now Sarah was anxious to know what the tests had shown.

'So how is he, Joyce?' she asked gently as the woman opened her nightgown.

'Fine. Dr Gillespie came back a short time ago to tell me that, physically at least, everything appears to be normal.'

Joyce smiled as she carefully settled the baby against her breast. She had been adamant from the outset that she wanted to breast-feed. She had done a lot of reading during her pregnancy and had decided for herself how important it was. While the midwives in the unit did all they could to encourage breast-feeding, they left the final decision to the individual mother.

Sarah agreed with this policy, hating the thought that a woman might be pressurised into doing something she didn't want to do. However, she knew how invaluable it was that a baby be put to the breast, if only for a short time after it was born, so that it could benefit from the vital antibodies and protein its mother produced.

'That's good. It must be a relief to know that,' she replied.

'It was. Both Ralph and I were so worried.' Joyce sighed as she looked at Sam, who was suckling greedily now, one tiny hand rhythmically kneading her breast in ecstasy. 'Of course, there could be other things wrong with him. He might be deaf, as a lot of Down's children are, and we don't know how much he'll be capable of learning.'

'But they've made huge advances in teaching methods with regard to children like Sam,' Sarah said encouragingly. She looked round as the door opened, feeling the heat flow along her veins as she saw that it was Niall.

'That's exactly what Dr Gillespie said!' Joyce laughed as she glanced from Sarah to the tall man standing by the door. 'Are you two in cahoots, then?'

'I'm not sure what you mean, Joyce.' Niall smiled easily as he came over to the bed and shot Sarah a quizzical look. 'What are you getting me into here, Sarah?'

'I was just saying to Joyce that teaching methods for Down's children have improved tremendously in recent years,' she explained a trifle shakily, trying to ignore the rush of pleasure she felt at having him speak to her in that warmly intimate tone. She summoned a smile but she couldn't prevent the tingling sensation from spreading through her whole body. 'E-evidently, you told her much the same thing.'

'I did,' he agreed quietly, his mouth curving into a pensive smile as he looked at her. 'Two minds with but one thought, would you say?'

She knew that it was just small talk yet that didn't stop her from feeling as though she and Niall were sharing some deeply significant moment...

He gave a deep laugh as he turned to Joyce. 'Or could it be that we're just telling you the truth? It's now widely accepted that a lot can be done to help Down's children lead fulfilling lives.'

Sarah didn't hear what Joyce said in reply. She

quickly made some excuse and left the room, strug-
gling to control a sense of disappointment which
almost overwhelmed her. What was the matter with
her? Why should she feel so let down just because
Niall hadn't meant anything by that chance remark?
He would have said the same thing to any colleague...

'Did I say something to upset you, Sarah?'

She swung round as Niall spoke softly behind
her. It was dark in the corridor with the lights
dimmed to their night-time setting. Sarah wondered
if it was that which made it so difficult to read his
expression before she realised that she was doing it
again, looking for something that wasn't there.

'No, of course not!' She gave a tinkly laugh,
which sounded too strained to be convincing, and
she saw him frown.

'Look, Sarah, if there is—' He stopped abruptly
as the lift doors opened and a porter appeared,
pushing Trisha on a trolley. Irene was there as well,
efficient as ever as she supervised the transfer to
the ward, yet Sarah was aware of the speculation
on her friend's face as she saw her and Niall together. The thought of the questions it might give
rise to later was more than she could bear!

'I—I have to go,' she said hurriedly. 'I want to
check on Ariel before I go back downstairs. It looks
as though we're in for a busy night.'

Niall didn't try to detain her as she hurried away.
But why should he? she thought wryly. As long as
she was doing her job efficiently, that was all he
was concerned about.

She paused outside the side room where Ariel

was receiving round-the-clock nursing care, aware that the thought caused her some pain, but she refused to try to work out why. She'd done enough soul-searching in the past few days! Now she had to remember what she had decided last night and concentrate on her work. It was unfortunate that she'd had run into Niall tonight but she had to get things into perspective—Niall Gillespie was a colleague and nothing more. She reached for the door handle, wishing she could feel more convinced of that!

The agency nurse who had been hired to special Ariel looked up as Sarah entered the room. 'Come to check on our patient, have you?' she asked in a whisper.

'Mmm, I thought I'd just pop in. How is she doing?' Sarah replied in the same quiet tone so as not to disturb the sleeping girl. She picked up Ariel's chart, unsurprised to find that the girl had been given diazepam intravenously for the past two days to control the effects of her eclampsia.

'Fine. Better than I expected when I first saw her. Poor kid was really ill then. However, her blood pressure has levelled off now, as you can see, and there's been no further sign of any convulsions.' The nurse yawned widely then laughed. 'In fact, I could do with more jobs like this. If you need anyone to be specialled again, put me at the top of the list! Mind you, I was surprised to be asked. I know what budgets are like at the moment. Whoever persuaded the management to pay for an agency nurse must be quite something.'

Sarah nodded, not trusting herself to say anything

in reply. She put the chart back on the end of the bed then left the room. She glanced along the corridor but Niall was nowhere in sight. She gave a heavy sigh as she thought about what the nurse had said so unwittingly. It was true. Niall Gillespie was very special indeed. That was part of the trouble!

'I hardly recognised you!' Sarah exclaimed in amazement as she spotted the young man walking along the corridor. She was at the end of her shift and had been on her way to the staffroom when she'd spotted Ariel's boyfriend, Jason. Now, as she stopped and took a good long look at him, she couldn't help marvelling at the changes.

Bathed and dressed in clean clothes, Jason bore little resemblance to the tattered figure he'd presented a few days earlier. Gone were the matted dreadlocks, his light brown hair standing in a fluffy halo of curls on top of his head. It gave him a curiously angelic appearance, Sarah thought, if you discounted the tattoos and studs in his ears, which he obviously hadn't been able to bring himself to get rid of!

Still, it was a vast improvement and said a lot that he was prepared to make such changes so that he could visit Ariel and his daughter. Sarah found herself warming to him.

'So, what are you doing here so early?' she asked as she walked along the corridor with him. 'It's too early to visit Ariel so have you come to see Star?'

'Yeah.' Jason grinned, although he looked faintly embarrassed, as if he wasn't too comfortable yet with his altered appearance. 'They let me hold her yesterday, just for a minute, mind. They said if I came back early this morning I might be able to give her a feed.' He shrugged with assumed non-chalance. 'I thought I'd give it a go, like.'

'Good for you!' Sarah replied encouragingly. 'Having you there will make all the difference to Star's progress. I popped in to see her during the night and the staff said that they are really pleased with how she is doing.'

She stopped outside the special-care unit to look through the glass window at the babies who were being cared for in there. There were five of them in all, tiny scraps wired to an array of machinery. Star was in the crib closest to the window and Sarah smiled as she saw how much better she looked.

Star had been fed through a nasogastric tube for the first few days and already her skin was losing its redness as she gained a little weight. Her tiny chest was moving steadily as she breathed in the oxygen which was flowing through a tiny catheter in her nostril. She was naked apart from a nappy and a knitted bonnet which helped retain her body heat.

Sarah could see a wisp of red hair poking out from under its brim, and she laughed in delight. 'So, where does she get the red hair from?'

Jason shuffled his feet. 'My mum,' he said shortly.

'And does she know about Star yet?' Sarah probed gently.

'No. She wouldn't be interested.' Jason's eyes were defiant but he couldn't quite disguise his hurt.

'She doesn't care about anything I do since she got married again.'

He gave her a tight smile then went and rang the bell. Sarah watched one of the nurses let him in and sighed as she carried on along the corridor. What a shame for everyone concerned if Jason was right. She couldn't imagine being part of a family like that. Although her own parents lived at the other end of the country, she knew that they were there if she needed them...

'Oh!' The breath whooshed from her body as she cannoned into a hard male form. For a moment Sarah teetered before two strong hands fastened themselves firmly on her shoulders.

'Are you all right?'

'I think so...' She took a deep breath but even that wasn't enough to fill her lungs as she stared up into Niall Gillespie's anxious face. She found herself wondering if there was enough air on the planet to stop her feeling so breathless...

She took one more desperate breath, her heart thundering as she struggled to regain her composure. 'I'm sorry. I didn't see you there.'

'So I realised.' His deep voice grated, the faint burr it held stroking roughly over her already sensitised nerves. Sarah shuddered as she felt ripples of sensation spread through her and knew at once that Niall had been aware of it as he suddenly let her go.

'I take it you're going off duty now?' he asked, still with that same oddly disturbing note in his voice.

'Y-yes. It's been a long night and I'm looking

forward to getting home to my bed.' She managed a smile, praying that he would put her nervousness down to tiredness. 'I'm sorry about bumping into you like that. I must watch where I'm going in future.'

'It doesn't matter,' he said impatiently, an odd expression crossing his face all of a sudden. 'Look, Sarah, I—'

'Sarah! Oh, great, glad I caught you.'

He stopped abruptly as Mike came hurrying along the corridor towards them. Even as she watched, Sarah could see his face settling into its usual chilly mask. Mike glanced uncertainly from her to Niall as he reached them.

'Sorry, I didn't mean to butt in but I was just wondering if you wanted a lift home, Sarah?'

'Yes. Thanks, Mike. That would be great.' Somehow she managed to keep her voice level but her heart was drumming inside her. She shot Niall a quick glance, wondering what he'd been about to say before they'd been interrupted. However, his expression gave nothing away as he quietly excused himself and headed off down the corridor.

'Ready, then? If you've had anything like the sort of night I've had then you must be dying to wipe the dust of this place off your dainty feet!'

Sarah took a deep breath. 'Too right! Lead on, McDuff, as they say!'

Mike laughed and looped his arm around her shoulders as they headed for the exit. Sarah responded to his teasing banter as best she could, glad that once they were astride his motorbike any further conversation was impossible. She closed her eyes as they rode through the town, wondering once again what Niall had been about to say...

She sighed wearily, realising that she was right back where she'd started eight hours before. She *had* to stop thinking about him all the time!

CHAPTER SIX

DESPITE how tired she was, Sarah found it impossible to sleep after she got home. She lay in bed for over an hour, tossing and turning, before finally getting up again. It was pointless to lie there when her mind was so active. Maybe a walk would help her unwind.

It was a little after nine when she left the house and took the path that led to the river. A small park had been made on the river bank with a section fenced off as a playground for the local children, although it was pretty empty at that time of the day.

She sat down on one of the swings and rocked gently back and forth, finding the motion soothing. Closing her eyes, she started to swing higher. The breeze tossed her blonde hair around and she smiled at the sense of freedom it gave her.

Maybe she was so on edge because she needed a holiday, she mused. It had been ages since she'd taken time out to do silly little things like swinging. When she was off duty her days were filled with all sorts of essential tasks, the hundred and one jobs that always needed doing around the house. Why if she set her mind to it, she couldn't remember the last time she'd spent a whole day doing nothing. It was no wonder she was so overwrought!

The swing flew higher as she thought about all the things she'd like to do if she had time. Walking and swimming, perhaps, or lounging about all morning, reading the newspapers and drinking coffee...

Her mouth tilted at the thought of such truly decadent pleasures and she swung even higher. There was something exhilarating about the rush skywards, followed by that heart-stopping plummet back towards the earth. Sarah gripped the chains tightly as the swing swooped and soared like a bird, laughing out loud in relief that she'd found such an easy explanation for the odd way she'd been acting recently. She needed a holiday. It was as simple as that!

'You're going to fly right up to the sun if you don't watch out. Then you'll get your wings burned.'

The teasing note in that familiar deep voice brought her back to reality with a rush. She opened her eyes and stared in shock at Niall Gillespie. He was lounging against one of the upright supports of the swing, his handsome face set into an expression that made her stomach feel as though a thousand butterflies had been set loose inside it.

She brought the swing to a stop while she struggled to find something to say, but it was impossible to sort through the jumble inside her head and make sense of it. It was only when she realised that he was holding Adair that she managed to speak.

'Are...are you going to fly her?' she asked through lips which felt as though they didn't really belong to her.

'Yes.' He glanced down at the bird and it seemed to Sarah that there was a roughness to his voice that hadn't been there a moment before. 'I couldn't sleep so I thought I might as well get a bit of fresh air while I had the chance.'

He looked up suddenly and his green eyes seemed to blaze as they looked into her hazel ones. 'Couldn't you sleep either, Sarah?'

'N-no.' She avoided his eyes as she slid off the swing, unsure what it was about the way he had looked at her that disturbed her so much. She gave a rueful little laugh, hoping it would disguise how she felt. 'I don't know why. Heaven knows, I was tired enough!'

'I know what you mean.' Niall sighed heavily. He gently adjusted the leather hood the bird was wearing before he looked at her again, and this time his expression held a wealth of weariness. 'Sometimes you can be tired to the point of exhaustion and yet it still isn't enough to free your mind of all the thoughts that plague you.'

The words described so perfectly how she'd felt that morning and yet she sensed he was alluding to something more than their joint inability to sleep that day. Her hands clenched as she wondered what he'd meant. She longed to ask him but the thought of the rebuff she might receive kept her silent.

'That sounded very philosophical, didn't it?' He gave a soft laugh, obviously wanting to lighten the mood a bit. 'And it's far too lovely a morning for that sort of thing. How do you fancy coming with me and trying your hand at flying this little lady?'

'Me? Oh, but I couldn't! Really, I have to get back...' she began, then felt a shiver run through her as she saw the warmth fade abruptly from his face.

'I apologise. I won't detain you any longer. Dawson must be wondering where you've got to.'

'Where I've got to...?' Sarah felt the ready colour flood her face as she suddenly grasped what he meant. 'Oh, Mike just gave me a ride home! He isn't... We don't...' She stopped as she realised what a hole she was digging for herself if she pursued that line.

'I see. Obviously I jumped to the wrong conclusion.' Niall's tone was level enough so she could only attribute the frisson which ran down her spine to embarrassment.

Had Niall honestly thought that she and Mike were sleeping together? she wondered shakily. Then she realised with a sinking heart that it was probably so. In this day and age it was quite acceptable behaviour. However, it wasn't acceptable to her, especially as she viewed Mike as a friend and nothing more. But the thought of explaining all that to Niall was more than she felt capable of right then!

'Well, I really must get back. I mean, there's tons of things I should be doing...' She bit her lip as she saw Niall's brows rise, not needing to see the look on his face to know how lame that had sounded. If she'd been asleep—as she should have been—then she wouldn't have been able to do any of those vitally important things!

She scuffed her toes across the rubber matting beneath the swing as she searched for an excuse that sounded convincing, but there simply wasn't one. Or none she could think of after being put on the spot like this!

'I suppose they could wait,' she admitted reluctantly.

'Do I take that as an agreement? You'll come?' Niall urged. 'Come on, Sarah, make that a definite yes!' He laughed at her continued hesitation, his voice holding a teasing note. 'I assure you that your reputation will be quite safe because we shall be properly chaperoned!'

'Chaperoned?' she repeated blankly. She stared at him in confusion and felt her heart lurch as he grinned at her. The smile lit up his whole face, making him look suddenly younger and even more handsome, she realised dazedly.

Her heart began to race as she started to notice all sorts of other things as well. He had shed his customary suit since he'd left work and he was as casually dressed as she was now, in jeans and a lightweight cream sweater, his feet laced into disreputable old trainers. The outfit didn't lessen his appeal in any way, though, she thought a shade desperately. If anything it increased it!

She knew that she was staring yet she couldn't seem to stop as her eyes ran helplessly over his lithely muscular body, taking stock of how the worn jeans clung to the contours of his powerful legs and fit so snugly about his narrow hips, lovingly cradling his masculinity...

Sarah took a quick breath and deliberately moved her gaze upwards, noting shakily how the sweater caressed his torso and strained across his shoulders. He obviously hadn't bothered to shave before coming out and the shadow of beard along his jaw gave him a rakish air, heightened by the way his dark hair fell in an unfamiliar tousled wave over his forehead.

It was Niall Gillespie but with a difference, she realised dizzily. Stripped of the usual trappings of conventionality—the immaculate suit and impeccable tie—there was a raw masculinity about the man who stood before her which awoke all sorts of dangerous feelings inside her.

It was only when she realised that Niall was making his own very thorough study of her that she finally looked away. She couldn't help the tremor that ran through her as she heard the awareness in his voice which the teasing words couldn't quite disguise.

'Adair will act as chaperone, Sarah. Believe me, with her about you couldn't be safer.'

'I never imagined for a moment...' she began, then stopped as he pressed a gentle finger to her lips. His eyes were as cool as the river that flowed past them yet his smile was so warmly tender that it filled her with heat.

'I was teasing, Sarah. So, will you come? Please? I'm sure you'll enjoy it. And I can't think of anything I would like more than to spend this beautiful morning with you and Adair.'

How could she refuse? Sarah knew that she couldn't resist the appeal she heard in his voice.

'All right, then. I will come. Thank you.' She managed to smile, trying to ignore the lingering sensation of warmth on her lips. It was just too disturbing to wonder why Niall should have this effect on her.

It was a relief when he turned and pointed towards the river, taking charge of the morning's proceedings with an easy friendliness which helped to quieten her fears as to the wisdom of what she was doing. After all, it *was* a beautiful morning. And she *did* want to see Adair fly. Why read any more into the invitation than that?

'We'll carry on along the river path if that's all right with you. There's a good spot to let Adair fly free not too far from here,' he suggested levelly.

'That's fine by me,' she replied, matching her tone to his.

She led the way down to the river and started along the path in the direction he'd indicated. The path narrowed after a few hundred yards, the overhanging trees filtering the sunlight to a soft greenish glow. There was little sound apart from the gurgling of the water as it flowed along beside them so that it felt as though she and Niall were suddenly cocooned in a private little world of their own.

Sarah walked on ahead, deeply conscious of the man following at her heels, but, then, all her senses seemed to be strangely heightened. The tangy scent of the moss and ferns which grew between the rocks was sharper than she'd ever recalled it, just as the air seemed even more moisture-laden as it misted on her skin. Fallen leaves had formed a soft mulch on the ground which deadened the sound of their footsteps, yet she could hear each step as though her hearing were super-tuned to the smallest sound.

Had Niall noticed it too? she wondered shakily. Did he feel as though he were suddenly seeing, smelling and hearing things more clearly than ever before?

'If you turn to your left just past that bush there's a path which leads up onto the hill. That's where we're heading.'

There was little in his voice to answer her questions and yet, with another of her highly tuned senses, she knew that it was so. Niall was experiencing everything she was, his senses more receptive than they had ever been. It shook her to realise it.

'Here we are.' He touched her arm to draw her attention to a gap in the trees. It was the lightest of contacts but she felt as though a firework had exploded inside her, sending out showers of red-hot sparks to set every cell in her body alight.

She took a deep breath as she turned blindly on to the path, willing herself not to betray how she felt. The path ended at a stile and beyond that the trees gave way to open country. Sarah climbed over the stile, deliberately pretending not to see his hand outstretched to help her. She jumped down on to the spring grass, forcing a smile as she turned to look at him, and felt her pulse leap as she saw the expression on his face, that faint but unmistakable hunger which made his eyes burn as though some of those sparks had set them alight, too!

'Up here, is it?' she asked huskily, shaken to her core by the sight. She turned to stare up the hill to where the green of the grass met the misty blue of the September sky while she tried to control the storm of emotions inside her. Had he really looked at her that way, with such…such longing?

'Yes. The air currents are stronger up there away from the trees. Adair can fly as high as she wants to then.'

His tone was completely impersonal as he imparted the information. Once that would have been enough to convince her that she'd been mistaken about what she'd seen on his face. Now, with her newly heightened perception, Sarah knew that it was merely a cover for his real feelings.

Niall might sound and act as coolly as he always did but beneath the ice a fire burned! And everything inside her screamed out a warning—danger! Danger!

'Are you coming, Sarah?'

He stopped and looked back when he realised that she wasn't following. Sarah took a deep breath. The sun was in her eyes so she couldn't see his expression now but that didn't matter. She knew what she had seen and heard. It scared her a little because she wasn't sure how to handle it. She should put an end to this right now, walk away and not look back, turn her back on the danger. Wasn't that the sensible thing to do?

Of course it was. It was just a pity that she wasn't going to take the sensible route! Sometimes there was just no other way but to step right into the heart of the fire—and risk getting burned!

'There! See, just over the top of those trees…yes!'

Sarah whooped with joy as Adair appeared above the tree line. She held her breath as the bird hovered overhead then swooped downwards in a spine-tingling descent. When she rose again Sarah gasped as she realised that Adair had something in her talons, a mouse or some such tiny rodent, which she carried off into the bushes to eat.

'That's fantastic,' she breathed. 'How on earth did she spot it from so high up?'

'I've no idea. It never fails to amaze me either.' Niall laughed at her enthusiasm. 'So, was it worth coming after all? You don't regret not rushing back to do the washing and ironing or some other vitally important task?'

The amusement in his voice made her laugh. 'Not at all. It's been marvellous. I can't remember when I last enjoyed a morning so much!'

'Good!' He gave her one last grin before he turned to call the bird back to him.

Sarah watched with a smile curving her mouth. What she'd said was true—the past two hours had been pure pleasure. Niall had done nothing to disturb her by a word or a look, if you discounted the fact that just being around him was disturbing! It made her wonder if she had read more into what had happened before than there had actually been?

She chased that thought from her mind as he slipped the hood back on the bird's head and turned round. 'Well, I suppose we'd better get back. I've a couple of patients to see this afternoon so I daren't play truant any longer.'

She laughed but she was surprised by what he'd said. 'Surely you aren't intending to go into work, today after being there all night long?'

He shrugged as he settled Adair on his arm and

began to lead the way back down the hill. 'I can't cancel appointments. It isn't fair to the patients to mess them around.'

'Surely it isn't fair to yourself to work both night and day, though? You can't spend all your life working, Niall,' she said softly.

He paused by the stile and his face was suddenly bleak. 'My work is my life, Sarah. It's as simple as that.'

He crossed the stile then stopped to offer her his hand to help her over. It was a good job he did because Sarah had no idea what happened next. Maybe she wasn't concentrating on what she was doing, her mind still mulling over what he'd said, but one minute she was climbing over the stile and the next she was falling forward.

'Careful!' Niall's cry of concern was almost drowned out by the bird's screech as she was summarily dislodged from his arm as he reached out to catch Sarah. He helped her to the ground then bent to look into her shocked face. 'Are you all right? You haven't hurt yourself?'

'Yes.' She gave a shaky laugh, her heart racing like crazy with the fright she'd had. 'Yes, I'm all right. And, no, I haven't hurt myself—that's what I'm trying to say.'

She summoned a smile as she looked up then felt it freeze on her lips as her gaze tangled with Niall's while the whole world seemed to come to a halt. She wasn't even aware of saying his name so that the sound of it coming from her lips shocked her, made her tremble with the force of feeling it unleashed. 'Niall…'

She saw his eyes darken with some sort of fierce emotion that made her breath catch. When he bent towards her she knew that he was going to kiss her and closed her eyes, making no attempt to evade the kiss. Maybe she'd known all along that this would happen...

His lips were cool against the warmth of hers, hard yet oddly gentle at the same time. It was such a strange juxtaposition—that hardness and soft-ness—that Sarah felt her mind spin as it tried to rationalise what was happening. She'd been kissed before, many times, but never like this. It scared her a little because she sensed it had the power to disturb her more than any other kiss had ever done.

She gave the softest murmur, not sure herself if it was of protest or pleasure, as she wondered if it was wise to let this go any further. She felt Niall tense as he sensed her hesitation before he abruptly started to draw back. And in that second she knew that wasn't what she wanted. She didn't want this kiss to end before it had really begun. She didn't want just half a memory to torment her with regrets but one whole beautiful memory to look back on with pleasure!

Her hand came up to cup the back of his head, her fingers burrowing into the cool silk of his dark hair as she stopped him from breaking off the kiss. She felt *his* hesitation this time, and with every scrap of her being willed him to do what she knew deep down he wanted to do.

'Oh, Sarah!'

Her name seemed to throb with a bitter-sweet sadness as it came from his lips. She had no time to work out what was behind it, though, before she felt his warm breath on her mouth, and then she lost all ability to think rationally. Instinctively her lips parted and she heard the soft groan he gave, mirrored it with her own as she felt the first gentle thrust of his tongue.

She drew his head down even more, feeling the hot surge of blood that raced through her body as Niall took charge with a mastery which thrilled her. His mouth was relentless as it took possession of hers time after time, that first light kiss turning into a raging torrent of kisses so that she felt giddy as the spate hit her—

Adair's sudden screech broke the spell with an abruptness that made Sarah's heart seem to leap into her throat. Her eyes were glazed as they opened to stare straight into Niall's...

She felt a chill invade her as she saw the anguish in his gaze. Her hand fell to her side as a searing pain lanced her heart. Did Niall regret what had happened? How could he?

'I'm sorry, Sarah. I never meant that to happen.' His voice grated harshly, the remorse it held leaving her in little doubt of his feelings.

She took a shuddering breath, willing herself not to cry. She wouldn't do that. It was bad enough that he should apologise, as though...as though those kisses were something to be ashamed of, without abasing herself any more!

'Don't worry about it, Niall. I won't.' She gave a dismissive shrug, wondering where she found the strength to lie when it felt as though her heart had been crushed to pulp. 'A few kisses are nothing to get upset about, are they?'

There was a moment when his eyes blazed, the anger in them shocking her with its intensity. Then he swung round and led the way back along the path, without uttering another word.

Sarah followed him in silence, not even trying to work out why he should be so angry. What did it matter now? She understood how he felt about kissing her and that was all she needed to know.

When it came down to it, Niall regretted that moment of weakness because he was still in love with the woman who'd let him down. What a pity she hadn't thought about that before she'd got herself well and truly burned!

'What on earth is going on in here?' Sarah demanded as she came into the ward. She looked round, taking in the scene that greeted her. Joyce Denning was hunched up on her bed, sobbing her heart out as she rocked Sam back and forth. The baby was wailing loudly, picking up his mother's distress, as babies often did.

Sarah put her hands on her hips as she turned to look at the other occupants of the ward. 'Well, I'm waiting. I want to know what's going on.'

'What do you think?' It was Trisha who piped up when neither of the other two women would answer. 'We don't want our kids catching what he's got! You had no right, putting him in here with normal babies!'

Sarah counted to ten but it didn't help. Maybe there was an excuse for such ignorance but for the

life of her she couldn't think of it! She treated each
of the women in turn to a look that scorched, before
turning her attention back to Trisha, who, she
guessed, was the instigator of this scene.

'Sam has Down's syndrome. It isn't contagious
and there's absolutely no danger to any of the babies
in this ward or in the rest of the maternity unit.'

'We only have *your* word for that.' Trisha
sniffed. 'It's a crime, putting a kid like that in here.
My Gary said so last night. He'll do something
about it even if you won't. He won't put up with
having a retard in here with his son!'

Sarah shot a glance over her shoulder, her heart
going out to poor Joyce. What must it be like for
the woman to be met with this sort of bigotry? She
turned back to Trisha, all the anger and frustration
which had been building up inside her since that
morning surfacing in a rush so that she saw the girl
blanch.

'I can only repeat what I've just told you—there
is no danger to any of the babies in this ward.
Down's is a genetic disorder. It doesn't result from
any form of disease so it can't be caught.
Understand?'

She turned to Joyce, not trusting herself to say
anything more. 'Why don't you come with me,
Joyce? I'll make you a cup of tea. Here, let me take
Sam for you.'

'No!' Joyce clutched the baby to her. She got up
and glanced around the room then walked to the
door, without saying another word.

Sarah followed her from the ward, glad to see

that the other two women were looking rather shame-faced. And so they should. There was no excuse for such behaviour in this day and age!

'Here, Joyce, sit down while I put the kettle on.' She gently guided Joyce to a chair in the staffroom then set about making the tea, glad when after a few minutes Joyce started to pull herself together. Sarah put the cup down on the table beside Joyce and smiled encouragingly.

'They just didn't understand, Joyce. Although that isn't much of an excuse, is it?'

'Oh, I don't know.' Joyce managed a smile. 'I suppose it's natural that they should worry. It's funny, because I knew that this could happen but it really knocked me for six when Trisha started muttering about me being in the ward with them.'

'I had a feeling she was the instigator,' Sarah sighed as she sipped her tea. 'All I can do is apologise. If we'd had any idea this would happen we would never have put her in the same ward as you.'

'It isn't your fault, Sarah. I don't suppose it's even Trisha's. This Gary fellow started it. I noticed him looking at Sam when he came visiting last night. It was obvious there was something on his mind even then. I suppose I'll have to get used to it.' Joyce sighed as she smoothed Sam's flushed cheek. 'Other people are bound to pass remarks so I'll just have to grow a thicker skin. Most people who knew that Sam was going to be handicapped thought Ralph and I were mad to go ahead and have the baby.'

'And are you sorry that you did?' Sarah said softly. 'Do you now regret not having a termination? Nobody would have blamed you if you had. It's understandable really.'

Joyce shook her head emphatically. 'No, I don't regret it at all. Maybe it's the right decision for a lot of women and I'm not trying to judge them. But it wasn't right for me or Ralph. Sam is still our son despite his handicap and we love him.'

'Then that's all that matters.' Sarah stood up. 'Now, what are we going to do? Do you want to remain in that ward, Joyce? Or would you prefer to move to another one?'

'Part of me says that I want to stay there because I don't want them thinking that I'm ashamed of Sam, while the other part of me just doesn't want to have to deal with any more unpleasantness,' she admitted.

'Then let me see about getting you moved. It will be better for both you and Sam in the long run. You really don't need this kind of upset right now,' Sarah said gently.

She left Joyce to finish her tea and went to find Irene to tell her what had happened. Irene shook her head in disbelief when she'd finished the tale.

'Would you credit anyone being so ignorant in this day and age? Poor Joyce, having to put up with that! Mind you, I expect she's right about it all being down to that boyfriend of Trisha's. One of the orderlies in Women's Surgical was only saying tonight that he's a bad lot.

'Evidently, he upped and left Trisha when she was six months pregnant. Went off with someone else, so I believe. It didn't last long, though. This other woman threw him out when he started getting violent. I suppose that's why he's reappeared in Trisha's life.'

'And why she's ready to agree with anything he says.' Sarah sighed. 'She's so desperate to hang on to him that she'll do anything to please him.'

'More than likely. Still, that doesn't help us, does it?' Irene frowned. 'I'm just trying to think where we can move Joyce to. We had five new admissions this afternoon and there are two mums in the delivery suite at the moment. We're bursting at the seams.'

'A real glut of babies!' Sarah laughed. 'Only to be expected in September. The end results of all that Christmas spirit!'

They both laughed because it was true. September was always a busy time of the year in the maternity unit. Irene gave a last chuckle then came up with a suggestion.

'How about putting Joyce in with Ariel? She's so much better now that I doubt it would cause any problems. And it is the only spare bed at the moment. I don't want to put Joyce in another ward and have this happen all over again if Trisha starts stirring up any more trouble.'

'Sounds like a good idea to me,' Sarah agreed.

'I think I should clear it with Dr Gillespie first, though. I believe he's still in his office so I'll give him a call, unless you want to do it,' she offered jokingly.

Sarah turned away, not trusting herself not to betray how that suggestion made her feel. The thought of speaking to Niall again after what had happened that morning was more than she could bear.

'Oh, I'll leave that honour to you, Irene,' she replied as lightly as she could. 'I'll just go and have a word with Joyce and tell her what we're planning.'

She left Irene to make the call but she couldn't deny how the thought of working with Niall in the coming weeks made her feel. Maybe he could dismiss what had happened between them that morning, but could she?

She touched a hand to her mouth, feeling the lingering echo of those kisses still imprinted on her flesh, and her heart sank.

It wasn't going to be easy to forget it!

CHAPTER SEVEN

'LAST turn on nights *and* Trisha Jackson will have gone by the time we come back on duty again.' Sally closed her locker with a flourish. 'Who said you can have too much of a good thing?'

Everyone laughed. Sarah popped her brush back into her bag and moved away from the mirror where she'd been tidying her hair, before going on duty. 'I saw Ann Baxter on my way in and she told me there had been a bit of a to-do in Trisha's ward this afternoon. Evidently the notorious Gary was shouting his head off and threatening to do all sorts of things. I don't know what it was all about because Ann didn't have time to tell me anything else.'

'Yes, I heard about it, too.' Irene sighed as she hung her jacket on a peg. 'Evidently Gary took exception to having a male midwife on the wards and started shouting the odds.'

'Typical! There are still some men who find it hard to accept the idea of a man as a midwife and yet they don't turn a hair when their partner is treated by a male doctor.' Sarah shrugged resignedly. 'I suppose it will take years to overcome their prejudice. It's such a shame, though, because you won't find anyone nicer than Dave Turner. The women who have him to deliver their babies all sing his praises. Anyway, what happened in the end? Who managed to sort things out?'

'Niall Gillespie. From what I heard, he gave Gary a real dressing down,' Irene replied.

'Rather him than me.' Sally grimaced. 'That Gary is trouble, if you want my opinion. It's a good job Dr Gillespie was around. Mind you, when isn't he? That man never seems to leave this place. He's here morning, noon and night. Looks to me as though he needs a good woman to give him a bit of TLC and take his mind off the job. Not that I'm hinting at anything, Sarah!'

Everyone laughed as they left the staffroom together. Sarah joined in, not wanting the others to know how that idea made her feel. Niall Gillespie had made it abundantly clear that he wasn't interested in any tender loving care she could give him!

Fortunately she had little time to dwell on that thought. As tended to happen all too frequently, they had two admissions almost at the same moment, and both of them promised to be difficult cases to deal with. Meena Patel was on duty again that night and she rolled her eyes in dismay.

'You can hardly credit that we would get two cases like this. I don't like the look of Hannah Jarvis at all. She's losing a lot of blood. I'd like to send her for an ultrasound as soon as possible to see what's going on.'

'There isn't anyone on duty in Radiology during the night.' Sarah frowned. 'Crazy situation, isn't it? I mean, these things don't just happen through the day. We need to be able to give scans twenty-four hours a day.'

'I know. It's something that needs sorting out,' Meena agreed. 'Maybe Niall can do something about it. He's in his office so would you give him a call and explain the situation to him, Sarah, please? In the meantime, I want Hannah Jarvis kept quiet in the hope that things might settle down, although I doubt it.

'As for the patient Deirdre Roberts brought in, I think a Caesarean section is inevitable. The baby is breech and the mother's water broke some time ago. She's having quite strong contractions but doesn't seem to be getting anywhere. I don't want to run the risk of pressure being put on the baby's cord, which will cut off its oxygen supply now that there isn't any fluid to cushion it.'

'Of course.' Sarah kept all inflection from her voice as Meena hurried away. She sighed as she headed for the office to make the call. In any other circumstances she wouldn't have given it a second thought but she felt deeply self-conscious about having to speak to Niall like this.

He answered his phone at the first ring and she felt her heart bump painfully as she heard his voice. 'Gillespie.'

'It's Staff Nurse Harris,' Sarah said carefully, desperate not to let him guess how difficult she found this. 'Dr Patel asked me to phone you. We have a patient here who's threatening to miscarry and Dr Patel feels that it would be helpful if we could arrange for an ultrasound scan.'

'And there's a problem about that?' His tone was completely neutral, making her wonder if he even remembered what had happened down by the river a few days earlier, let alone thought about it the number of times she had!

The thought was just what she needed to steady her, however. 'The radiology unit isn't open at night, Dr Gillespie,' she explained with chilly politeness.

'Surely there's some provision for this sort of emergency?' The anger that tinged his voice brought it instantly to life, but, then, this situation centred on the welfare of one of his patients. It was his job to feel concerned about them, to want to give of his best where his work was concerned. Hadn't he told her that just before he'd kissed her, that his work was his life? Now Sarah was beginning to understand that he'd meant what he'd said!

'I believe a radiologist can be called in if it's deemed absolutely essential,' she explained quietly. 'However, it's frowned on by the management because of the costs it incurs.'

'To hell with the cost! What point is there in having equipment lying idle when it's needed most?' His deep voice rippled with passion and Sarah closed her eyes on a wave of helpless longing. If only Niall would show just a little of that passion in his private life! If he would let down the barriers maybe there was a way to convince him that love needn't be a painful experience...

'Sarah...are you still there?'

There was a moment, one foolish, crazy second, when her heart swelled as she heard the concern in his voice. Then she realised with a cold return of sanity that he was concerned because they hadn't resolved this situation.

Tears stung her eyes but she forced herself to concentrate on what was being said, not on what she *wanted* to hear. 'Yes, of course. What would you like me to do, Doctor?'

He didn't answer for a moment, almost as though he'd sensed her distress and was puzzled by it. Then his voice came clearly over the line, cool, controlled, professional to a fault, all the proof she needed that her needs came a poor second to those of his patients. 'I shall deal with this myself, Staff. Tell Dr Patel that I shall make all the arrangements necessary. Thank you.'

The line went dead. Sarah slowly replaced the receiver with a heavy heart. It appeared that everything had been said.

'Shh, shh, Hannah. It's all right. Everything is going to be all right, love.' Sarah sat on the edge of the bed, rocking the girl in her arms. She felt so helpless in the face of Hannah Jarvis's grief. All she could do was offer what comfort she could, but it was all too little.

The ultrasound scan had shown that Hannah had already lost her baby. Unfortunately, though, most of the placenta had been left behind after she'd miscarried. Now it would need to be removed as soon as possible to avoid any future complications.

'Come on now, wipe your eyes.' Sarah handed the sobbing girl a wad of tissues and waited while she blew her nose. She looked round as the door opened then looked away immediately when she saw it was Niall.

He came straight over to the bed and stood, looking down at Hannah with gentle sympathy in his eyes. 'I'm so sorry about this, Hannah. I wish we could have done something but it was too late.'

'I know.' Hannah sniffed but tears were still welling from her eyes. 'They told me that the baby was...gone.'

'That's right. Now we need to evacuate your uterus and get rid of the remains of the placenta. It will be done under a general anaesthetic so you won't feel anything,' Niall explained in the same gentle tone.

'Was it something I did, Doctor? I went swimming today. Could that have caused it to happen?' Hannah's face contorted with grief and guilt. 'I thought it would be good for me to try to keep fit but maybe that triggered things off.'

'No. It was just one of those unfortunate things, Hannah. Something we have no control over, I'm afraid,' Niall said quietly, sounding strained. Sarah cast him a quick glance, wondering at the sudden expression of pain that crossed his face. She knew how much he empathised with his patients but his distress seemed almost personal...

She pushed aside that strange idea, turning her thoughts back to what was happening and determinedly keeping them there as Niall addressed her. 'Hannah will be going down to Theatre straight away. I shall handle this myself and I want you to assist me, Staff, if you would.'

'Certainly.' Sarah gave Hannah one last encouraging hug then stood up. 'I'll get everything ready.'

'Thank you.' Niall left the room, leaving her to prepare Hannah for the operation. It was a simple enough procedure but the reason for doing it was the most painful thing of all.

Hannah's husband, Chris, arrived just before she went down to Theatre. He had been away on business and had come rushing back after Hannah had phoned him at his hotel. Sarah left them alone for a few minutes to give them chance to grieve together for the loss of their baby. It was one aspect of the job she hated and had never come to terms with.

She made her way to the office to afford them some privacy while she wrote up Hannah's notes. She was surprised to find Deirdre Roberts, one of the community midwives, there when she opened the door. However, all it took was one look at Deirdre's face to tell her that something was wrong, and she mentally crossed her fingers that nothing had happened to the patient Deirdre had brought in earlier, the woman having the breech baby.

'Are you all right, Deirdre?' she asked as she closed the door on the bustle outside.

'Oh, I suppose so.' Deirdre grimaced. 'I'm still in one piece at least!'

'What do you mean?'

'Oh, Dr Gillespie just tore a strip off me. He virtually accused me of incompetence!' Deirdre tried to smile but Sarah could see that she was upset, and no wonder!

In line with many maternity units, Dalverston operated a system whereby a community midwife could bring a patient into hospital just for the birth. The mother would stay only a few hours afterwards then return home as long as she and the baby were both well.

Sarah had met Deirdre many times because of this system and had nothing but respect for her work. She couldn't begin to understand why Niall had made such an accusation.

'Why on earth did he say that, Deirdre?' she queried in confusion.

'Because of Angela Murray—the breech?' Deirdre continued once she was sure Sarah knew whom she was referring to. 'I suppose I can understand it in a way, but Dr Gillespie never gave me a chance to explain the situation properly. He just let rip in that very icy way he has. I think it would have been almost better if he'd sounded angry!'

Sarah knew what she meant! It wasn't that long ago since she'd been treated to Niall's cold displeasure...

Her mind made a sudden leap back to that time beside the river when he'd kissed her with such passion. He hadn't been cold then, though!

She cut short that thought, although she could feel the heat creeping into her cheeks at the memory. 'So what did happen tonight? Did you know the baby was going to be breech?'

'Oh, yes. And I explained to Angela that she would need to come into hospital even though she'd elected a home birth. Maybe I should have kept quiet and just sprung it on her then we wouldn't have had this problem!'

'Sounds a bit drastic!' Sarah laughed. 'I take it

that Mrs Murray wasn't keen on being admitted to hospital?'

'That's an understatement!' Deirdre groaned. 'Evidently she had a dreadful time when her first child was born. The hospital where she was admitted was one of those places where no account is taken of the mother's wishes. Angela said that she felt as though she were on a conveyor belt. Everything had to be done to a set routine and that was it.

'She'd set her heart on a home birth this time and there were no problems until we realised that the baby was presenting as breech.'

'Didn't they try to turn it?' Sarah queried.

'Yes, last week. The doctor tried external version but the baby turned itself round again a few hours later. I told Angela then that she would need to come into hospital, although I did explain that she need only stay a few hours as long as everything went smoothly.' Deirdre sighed.

'I could tell she wasn't happy about the idea. I imagine that's why she didn't phone me tonight until her water had broken. She probably thought that once everything was under way she'd get her wish to stay at home. However, by the time I saw her it was obvious that the baby was becoming distressed. I got her here as fast as possible.'

'You did all you could, Deirdre,' Sarah assured her. 'You weren't to know she'd do such a silly thing.'

'Oh, I know that! But Dr Gillespie didn't give me a chance to explain my side of it.' Deirdre smiled wanly. 'Still, at least everything turned out all right in the end. Angela had a little girl and both she and the baby are fine. I suppose that's all that matters at the end of the day.'

'Of course,' Sarah agreed, although it didn't seem fair that Niall should have been so hard on Deirdre when she hadn't been at fault.

She set about writing up Hannah's notes after Deirdre left, then went back to take Hannah down to Theatre. Hannah's husband intended to wait while the operation was done and she didn't try to dissuade him. At a time like this the young couple needed one another more than ever in her view.

Niall was scrubbing up when she delivered Hannah into the care of the anaesthetist, and he glanced round as she went into the scrub room. 'How's she doing?' he asked levelly.

'So-so.' Sarah started her preparations, methodically scrubbing her hands and forearms with antiseptic soap, before donning a sterile cotton gown. 'Her husband has arrived and is going to wait until she gets back from Theatre.'

'Good. She needs all the support she can get at the moment,' he agreed. 'I think we should offer them counselling if they're interested. It might help them get over this.'

'Of course. There's a good support system for cases like this, which Dr Henderson set up.' Sarah hesitated, wondering if she should mention to him how upset Deirdre Roberts was.

'Something on your mind?' He seemed to have guessed something was bothering her. He raised his brows when she didn't answer immediately. 'Come on, out with it, Sarah. You may be an excellent nurse but you're no good at hiding your feelings!'

She felt herself flush at that. She wasn't sure she liked the idea that he could read her mind in view of how mixed up she'd felt lately! She avoided his eyes as she concentrated on tucking her hair into the disposable hood.

'Deirdre Roberts is very upset about what you said to her earlier. Evidently you didn't give her chance to explain the situation properly.'

'What is there to explain?' Niall's tone was harsh. 'There's never an excuse for putting a patient at risk.'

'That isn't fair!' she retorted, stung by his refusal to listen. 'Angela Murray *knew* that her baby was breech, but she was so determined she wasn't going to come into hospital that she didn't phone Deirdre until after her water had broken. There was nothing Deirdre could have done about it.'

'Which simply proves that mothers should be discouraged from opting for a home birth in the first place. What point is there in taking even the smallest risk when there's no need?' He didn't wait for her to answer, turning to lead the way into the theatre and effectively putting an end to the conversation.

She followed him slowly, wondering what had made him so intransigent in his views. She sighed as her eyes rested wistfully on the back of his dark head. She had the feeling that he wouldn't tell her even if she asked. That would mean crossing those invisible boundary lines he had drawn between himself and the world!

* * *

'Well, I've finally gone and done it! As of the twentieth of September I'm a free woman!'

Sarah put down her magazine as Irene came into the staffroom and made the announcement. She'd been snatching a break while there was a lull. Now she raised her brows as she looked at her friend.

'I'd say that needs a bit of explaining, Sister Prentice. So, come on…give!'

Irene grinned. 'Oh, it's simple really. I've just handed in my notice…or rather I've left it in the tray for Elaine Roberts to get in the morning. I haven't taken any holidays this year so that means I'll be able to leave in two weeks' time!'

'Lucky you!' Sally Green stood up and stretched. 'Think about it, lazing around all day, not having to deal with people like Trisha…Oh, boy, bliss!'

Sarah laughed. 'You know you love every minute of it! Anyway, if it's what you want, Irene, good for you. But we can't let you leave without a good send-off. We'll have to organise a party or something.'

'It's all sorted out,' Irene informed them triumphantly. 'How about us all going over to Ulverston for their Lantern Procession? They usually hold it on the second or third Saturday in September so the timing couldn't be better. Then you're all invited back to my place afterwards for a party!'

'Sounds great to me!' Helen said, voicing everyone's view. 'I've heard about the Lantern Procession but I've never seen it.'

'You don't know what you're missing,' Sarah informed her. 'I've only managed to get there once because I've always been working but it's quite spectacular. You'll love it.'

'You will. And so will Bob,' Irene added, referring to Helen's boyfriend. 'Bring him along, too. Everyone's invited—' She broke off and smiled as she looked towards the door. 'Hello, Dr Gillespie, I didn't notice you there. We were just sorting out my retirement party.'

'So you've set the date now, have you, Irene? You'll be sorely missed, I must say.'

Sarah kept her eyes focused on the dregs of tea in the bottom of her cup, trying to ignore the quiver which ran through her as she realised Niall was in the room. She didn't look up, even when she heard his footsteps coming closer, yet she knew the very moment he stopped behind her chair. It wasn't anything physical because he didn't touch her—she just knew he was there and her heart thundered painfully as she realised how foolishly she was behaving.

Niall had no real interest in her. So maybe he *had* kissed her the other morning, held her as though for a few desperate moments he hadn't wanted to let her go, but that had been some sort of...of temporary aberration on his part. The real truth was that Niall was as indifferent to her as he was to every woman—except the one who had hurt him so badly!

'So, what are you planning to do to mark your retirement?' Niall's voice held friendly interest and the faintly constrained atmosphere which had descended with his arrival disappeared at once.

'Irene has come up the idea of us all going over

to Ulverston to watch their Lantern Procession,' Sally chipped in, as irrepressible as ever. 'Then it's back to her house afterwards for the party of the year!'

Everyone laughed, Niall included. He rested his hands on the back of Sarah's chair so that his knuckles brushed the nape of her neck. She bit her lip to contain the shock of awareness that raced through her veins like lightning, but it was impossible to ignore the tantalising touch of his fingers even though she was sure he was unaware of it.

'Sounds good to me. Is it an open invitation?' he queried levelly, though Sarah fancied she detected a hint of strain beneath the lightly spoken words. The urge to look at him became so strong that she almost gave in to it, but somehow she managed to resist. It would serve no purpose, looking for something which didn't exist.

'Of course! I hope that means you'll come, Dr Gillespie. If you haven't seen the procession, that alone is worth the trip. And you're more than welcome to come back to my house afterwards to join in the party,' Irene offered immediately.

'Thank you. I appreciate the invitation.' He didn't add anything more so that Sarah had no idea whether or not he intended to accept. He straightened up and she felt a sudden chill invade her as the warmth of his fingers disappeared.

'I won't keep you all from your well-earned breaks. However, I just wanted to say that I have apologised to Deirdre Roberts. Some of you might know that I was a bit quick to criticise her handling of the Angela Murray case. However, I realise now that Deirdre wasn't to blame in any way and I've made certain she understands that I have complete confidence in her professional judgement.' He gave them all a cool smile then left the room as quietly as he had appeared.

It was Sally Green who voiced everyone's surprise. 'Well, that's a turn-up for the book! I wouldn't have expected our Dr Gillespie ever to concede that he might have made a mistake.' She sighed theatrically. 'My, my, but he's almost too perfect, isn't he? Handsome, dedicated, sexy as sin... Makes me almost wish I weren't happily married!'

Everyone laughed before they carried on making plans for the night out. Sarah listened to the chatter but she didn't join in. There was a small glow somewhere in the region of her heart, warm and oddly comforting. If Niall could admit that he'd been wrong about one thing, maybe he wasn't a completely lost cause. Maybe it would be possible to make him understand that he might also be mistaken about other things as well, like his refusal to let anyone get close to him ever again...

'You're looking very smug, Sarah Harris. What are you planning?'

'Nothing!' Sarah laughed off the question, ignoring the disbelieving look Irene treated her to. It hadn't been a lie because it wasn't a plan exactly. That warm little glow hadn't progressed to that point yet. But it was something to think about all right...a beginning rather than a dead end!

CHAPTER EIGHT

THE rest of the night passed quietly enough, apart from one rather strange incident. Sarah was transferring a patient to the wards in the early hours of the morning. It had been a routine delivery and all the new mum needed now was a few hours' sleep.

After quietly instructing the exhausted woman to ring the bell if she needed anything, Sarah left the ward. There was half an hour to go before she went off duty, just enough time to write up the case notes and get ready to hand over to the day staff.

Irene usually performed that task but she was assisting at another birth so Sarah would take over the job for her. She was just about to go into the office and sort things out when the door was opened from the inside and Trisha appeared.

There was a moment of surprised silence before Sarah found her voice. 'What's going on, Trisha? Why were you in the office? You know patients aren't allowed in there without a member of staff.'

'Sorry. I just…just needed to make a phone call,' Trisha explained hurriedly. She glanced along the dimly lit corridor, studiously avoiding Sarah's eyes.

'At this time of the morning?' Sarah didn't try to disguise her disbelief. She stepped around Trisha and took a good look round the room, but everything seemed in order, the papers on top of the desk undisturbed, from what she could tell, the drug cupboard locked as it always was.

She shot the girl another searching look, noticing immediately that Trisha seemed rather agitated. Was it guilt because she knew that she shouldn't have gone into the office under any circumstances? Or because she was lying about her reasons for doing so? It was impossible to tell.

'Look, I'm sorry. I know I shouldn't have gone in there but I just needed to phone Gary. OK?' Trisha stated with a mounting belligerence in her tone. 'You can see I haven't touched anything!'

Sarah sighed. So once again Gary was at the back of this, albeit indirectly. She decided that there was no point in making a fuss and risk having the rest of the patients disturbed. Trisha was being discharged the following day so that would be the end of her—and Gary—thankfully!

She waited until Trisha had returned to her ward then went into the office and made a thorough check of all the drawers and cupboards, but nothing appeared to have been disturbed. It seemed that Trisha had been telling the truth, although why she'd needed to phone Gary so urgently was another story. However, Sarah decided that it was one she didn't want to hear. Frankly, she'd had quite enough of both of them!

She wrote up the case notes then handed over to the day staff when they arrived and left the hospital with a sigh of relief. She wasn't sorry to get to the end of this shift. She could only hope things would be easier when she came back on duty in a few days' time. It wasn't the work which was bothering her, however, but something else entirely…six feet of dark-haired, infuriatingly attractive male answering to the name of Gillespie, to be precise!

Determined to carry out her plan to take some time for herself, Sarah did the minimum amount of housework in the next three days while she was off duty. Instead, she filled her time with treats, like going swimming and reading the papers from cover to cover, or taking long walks because the weather was still gloriously warm and sunny.

She even went back to the river and followed the path she and Niall had taken that morning, but she found surprisingly little pleasure in doing so. There were too many reminders of what had happened there, too many questions as to why Niall had kissed her in the first place.

Had it been an impulse he couldn't control? Would it have happened if he'd been with any woman and not just with her? She was afraid that might be a little too close to the truth.

She returned to work, feeling less relaxed by the break than she'd hoped. The only consolation was that Niall was tied up in meetings as plans for the new maternity unit were thrashed out with the area health authority. At least she didn't have to risk bumping into him all the time, she consoled herself, then realised after the first few hours that she missed seeing him around. She really couldn't win!

It was a relief to discover that the hectic spell hadn't abated. At least while she was busy there was less time to brood. There were new mums being admitted all the time and others being discharged. Trisha had gone—thankfully—and so had Joyce Denning, whom everyone missed, especially Ariel, who still wasn't well enough to be discharged. Sarah went into her room just before lunch and found the girl staring wistfully out of the window.

'So, how are you feeling?' she asked, noticing the girl's drooping posture immediately. Ariel looked depressed and unhappy, and she made a mental note to speak to Meena about her.

All the staff were aware of how easily a mother could lapse into post-partum depression. This was partly due to a sudden feeling of anticlimax after the birth and all the build-up to it, and partly due to hormonal changes. Ariel needed to have a careful eye kept on her, just in case.

'All right, I suppose. It will be another week at least before I can leave, so Dr Patel said this morning,' Ariel sighed as she stared moodily out of the window again. 'I wish I could take Star with me but she still isn't well enough to leave the special care unit.'

'It won't be long now, though,' Sarah said encouragingly. 'She's making wonderful progress, considering how underweight she was at birth.'

'I know. If I'd had any idea…' Ariel bit her lip as tears welled into her eyes.

'You mustn't keep blaming yourself. It won't do any good.' She went over and gave the girl a hug. 'You have to concentrate on getting yourself one hundred per cent fit so that when Star *is* allowed to leave hospital you'll be well enough to look after her.

'That's what Dr Gillespie said yesterday.' Ariel didn't appear to notice how Sarah stiffened at the mention of his name. 'He said that I must take care of myself for Star's sake.'

'And, of course, he was right.' Sarah heard the clipped note in her voice but she couldn't help it. She moved away from the window and picked up Ariel's chart, concentrating on what it contained rather than the foolish way her heart was racing at the mere mention of Niall's name.

On the plus side, Ariel's blood pressure was back to normal and there had been no sign of any more fits. However, she was being monitored for kidney damage, as eclampsia could have a profound effect on the kidneys. Urine and blood samples had shown some cause for concern, making it essential that Ariel remain in hospital a while longer. What the long-term prognosis would be was as yet unknown but Sarah knew that Ariel would need to be closely monitored for some time.

She put the chart down and went back to slide a comforting arm around the girl's thin shoulders. 'You must try being positive and think about what you're going to do when you leave here. You know that it wouldn't be wise to take Star to the camp because she's going to need a lot of care for the first few months, so have you made any plans yet? Is there anyone who will help you—your family, for instance?'

'No. I don't have any family. I was brought up in a children's home.' Ariel scrubbed away her tears with the back of her hand, making a determined effort to overcome her blues. 'But Jason and

I were talking about it last night and we've decided to accept Joyce's offer until we can find a place of our own. She said that we can stay with her when I leave hospital. Ralph runs a print shop and he's offered Jason a job there. He's going to give it a try, anyway.'

'Why, that's wonderful!' Sarah exclaimed, thinking how well things had turned out. Moving Joyce into Ariel's room, it had worked out better than anyone could have hoped. The pair had struck up an instant friendship, undoubtedly aided by the fact that Ariel had accepted Sam's condition without question.

She was still smiling as she made her way along the corridor a few minutes later. It was nice to know that something good had come out of that unpleasant episode. She glanced at her watch as she passed the staffroom, realising in surprise that it was lunchtime already. She had brought sandwiches with her and, on a sudden impulse, decided to take them outside into the garden as it was such a lovely warm day.

She had just settled herself on a bench when she heard footsteps coming along the gravel path. She glanced round and felt her heart lift, like a bird taking flight, when she saw Niall. He paused when he spotted her sitting on the bench. It was only the briefest of hesitations but enough to make her suspect that he wasn't pleased to see her there.

She looked down, making a great performance out of unpacking her sandwiches so that he wouldn't feel he had to stop and speak to her when it was obvious how much he disliked the idea!

'Sarah?' There was a hint of a question in his deep voice, mingled with a thread of wary amusement. She kept her gaze locked on the package in her lap, concentrating on peeling open the layers of cling film. She didn't want to look into those cool green eyes and see what she expected to see…

'Look at me, Sarah.' Niall's voice was firm, the hand that reached out and lifted the packet of sandwiches from her knee as steady as a rock.

She swallowed the little knot of pain lodged in her throat as she struggled to find something witty to say, something to make Dr Niall Gillespie understand that she didn't *care* how he felt about her! Her lips were just about to form the first frosty syllable when that rock-steady hand moved to her chin and tilted it so that she was forced to meet that cool green stare after all—only it wasn't as cool as she'd imagined it would be!

There was a short silence which seemed to hum even without any words to fill it. Sarah felt her heart come to a complete stop as she wondered what she could see in Niall's eyes at that moment. And then, before she could work it out, he looked away as his hand dropped to his side, leaving her feeling bereft and aching for something she barely understood.

'This has to do with what happened the other day by the river, hasn't it, Sarah?'

His voice grated, the way he thrust back his hair proof of his impatience. In a way she couldn't blame him for feeling that way. It had been just a few kisses, that was all. Nothing more than that. Why go on trying to read more into what had happened than had been intended?

'I don't know what you mean—' she began, embarrassed by her inability to treat the incident as casually as he obviously did.

'Don't! Please, don't lie to me, Sarah. That, coming on top of everything else, is more than I can stand.'

On top of everything else? What did he mean? For a blank second Sarah stared at him in confusion, seeing the anguish that contorted his features without understanding its cause. And then it came to her in a jolt of cold comprehension, which brought her to her feet in a rush.

'I apologise, Niall,' she bit out, the contempt in her voice barely concealing her pain. 'I didn't realise that you'd feel so *guilty* about what happened!'

'Guilty?' He took a half-step toward her, coming so close that their bodies almost touched. Sarah felt the instant stir of awareness which ran through her veins like some potent drug, bringing every nerve to tingling life. It was only when he repeated the question that she forced herself to concentrate on what she'd started. She knew immediately that she didn't want to continue this conversation!

'Guilty? What the hell is that supposed to mean?' he demanded harshly.

'Nothing. Forget I said that. I…I didn't mean it.' She tried to walk past him but he was too quick for her. His hands clamped on her upper arms, bringing her to a jolting halt so that her body swayed towards his before she could stop it.

There was a moment when she let herself lean against him as the warmth and strength of his body came into contact with the softness of hers, and then she was pushing herself away from him and hurrying along the path. He called her name, just once, his voice barely carrying above the sound of her footsteps on the gravel, but she didn't stop.

What was the point? What could she say to him? That she was as sorry as he was about what had happened down by the river that day?

She choked back a bitter laugh as she stepped inside the building. It would be a lie! And Niall had said that he didn't want her to lie to him. But the alternative, to tell him that those kisses had haunted her and would continue to do so, was something he wouldn't want to hear either.

'Right, so everyone's clear what to do?' Irene glanced around at the assembled group. 'We're bound to get split up in this crowd so once the procession is over everyone is to make his or her way back to the cars by…what? Say, ten o'clock at the latest?'

'Why don't we synchronise watches?' Helen piped up, grinning cheekily. 'That way you can be sure we'll all be on time!'

'Cheeky young madam!' Irene aimed a good-natured clip at Helen's ear, laughing as the girl neatly dodged out of the way. 'I'm only trying to make sure you all get your fair share of the buffet I've made. I *know* what you lot are like, first come scoffs the lot! Still, you only have yourselves to blame!'

Everyone laughed before they all began to make their way towards the route the Lantern Procession was going to follow as it wended its way through

Ulverston town centre. Sarah had been surprised to see how many people had turned up for Irene's retirement do. Now she spotted several more faces she knew, joining their party. Everyone was laughing and joking as they made their way to the centre of the town, obviously having fun.

She wished she felt more like joining in but she'd only come along because Irene would have been hurt if she hadn't made the effort. Since that encounter with Niall in the garden two weeks previously, she hadn't seemed to be able to summon up much enthusiasm for anything.

'Are you sure you're all right, Sarah, love? You aren't sickening for anything, are you?'

She summoned a smile as she heard the concern in Irene's voice. 'Not that I know of! No, I'm just a bit run-down, I think.'

'Sure?' Irene glanced over her shoulder and waved to her husband, who was waiting for her to join him. She turned back to Sarah again and frowned. 'I've noticed how quiet you've been lately. If anything is worrying you, you know you can talk to me, don't you?'

'Yes. Thanks, Irene.' It was an effort to hold the smile but she managed it. 'As I say, I think I'm just a bit tired. Maybe I'll book myself a holiday.'

'Good idea. Some place hot. Lots of sun, sea, sand and—'

'I get the picture!' Sarah laughed a shade too heartily, not wanting Irene to guess how that idea made her feel. The only person she was interested in *that* way didn't want to know she even existed!

She glanced around, looking for an excuse to escape from any more well-meaning advice. 'Oh, look, there's Mike. I'll just go and catch him up. See you later.'

She hurried off, without waiting for Irene to reply, but once out of sight of her friend she immediately changed direction. The last thing she wanted was to spend the evening with Mike and be made to feel guilty. He'd asked her out several times in the past couple of weeks but each time she'd turned him down. It wasn't fair to let Mike go on hoping for something that could never be, but he seemed impervious to the hints she'd been giving him.

She was soon swallowed up by the huge crowd which had gathered to watch and take part in the procession. There were lanterns of all shapes and sizes being waved about, some of them so intricate in design that it was hard to believe they were made out of willow canes and white tissue paper all held together with glue and tape.

A lot of the local children attended the workshops in the weeks before the procession and had fun, making their own lanterns. Now the results of their efforts were being proudly carried aloft, the candles inside each lantern glowing against the night sky.

There was a pervading air of excitement everywhere, but Sarah felt oddly detached from the revelry. It was as though lately she had lost her ability to enjoy even the simplest pleasures. Mercifully, Niall had been so heavily involved in the expansion plans that his time in the maternity unit had been limited to consultations.

She had assisted him at each session, taking care

that she never once let her feelings show. Not that he had ever once alluded to what had happened but, then, she hadn't given him any opening to do so either! Getting into a discussion about what she'd meant when she'd accused him of feeling guilty, that wasn't something she intended to do.

'Sarah... Hey, Sarah!'

She stopped as she heard someone calling her. She glanced round, her face breaking into a smile as she spotted Laura and Ian making their way through the crush towards her. She barely had a chance to say hello to them before a small body hurled itself at her, and she laughed as she lifted Robbie high into the air and gave him a hug.

'Well, hi, there, sunshine!' She gave the small boy a kiss, laughing as he hugged her tightly around the neck. Robbie loved everyone he met and let them know it.

'You're going to strangle poor Sarah like that. Come here!' Laura lifted her son out of Sarah's arms and laughed. 'What a greeting. But it proves it's been too long since we saw you last. What have you been up to?'

'Oh, nothing much. Hello, Ian. How are you?' Sarah asked as Laura's husband finally made it through the crush of people and joined them. He was holding a lantern on the end of a long pole and she frowned as she tried to work out what it was supposed to represent.

'It's a car,' Ian explained helpfully. 'Robbie made it all by himself.'

'Well, it's lovely. Aren't you a clever boy, then?' She laughed as she ruffled Robbie's hair, then felt her lips freeze as she saw the man who had come up behind her friends. For a moment Laura and Ian and the whole crowd seemed to disappear as she stared at Niall...

She took a deep breath and everything suddenly shot back into focus: Robbie's laughing face, Laura's questioning frown as she turned to see what had caught her attention, how it suddenly changed to tentative recognition...

'I hope I'm not interrupting.' Niall apologised as he joined them. 'However, I just happened to spot Sarah. I need a quick word with her, if you don't mind. I'm Niall Gillespie, by the way. I'm the new consultant obstetrician at the hospital.'

'Nice to meet you,' Ian said, holding out his hand and smiling pleasantly as he made the introductions. 'I'm Ian Grady and this is my wife, Laura. And this young man is Robbie.'

'Oh, I've heard all about Robbie. He has quite a fan club at the hospital!' Niall laughed as Robbie suddenly launched himself towards him. He took the child into his arms and grinned at him. 'Hi, Robbie. I'm Niall.'

'Niya...' Robbie struggled with the unfamiliar name, obviously delighted to have found yet another friend. He was unaware of the small silence which had fallen, but Sarah was keenly conscious of it. She glanced at Laura and was surprised by the frowning look she was giving Niall.

'I have the strangest feeling that I've seen you somewhere before,' Laura suddenly blurted out, then laughed in embarrassment. 'It's a good job I'm a happily married woman or you could take that the wrong way!'

'I could only wish!' Niall replied, smiling at her. 'However, I'm sure I would have remembered if we had met before, Laura,' he added gallantly, yet Sarah noticed a sudden tension about him. It aroused her curiosity immediately. What was wrong with Niall? Why did it seem to bother him that Laura thought she'd recognised him?

She had no time to work it out because he turned to her just then. 'What time is everyone meeting up to go back to Irene's house? I forgot to ask.'

'Te-ten o'clock,' she mumbled, her heart sinking. She'd had no idea that he would be there tonight. Now the thought of an evening spent in such close proximity with him made her mind race as she searched for a way out.

'I'll see you there then, I expect.' He gave her a last cool smile before he handed Robbie back to his mother, but there seemed to be the faintest hint of challenge in it. Sarah watched him threading his way through the crowd, wondering if there was any way she could get out of going to the party...

'I wish I could remember where I've seen him before,' Laura said with a sigh. 'I thought his name was familiar when I first heard it mentioned, but for the life of me I can't remember why. It's so infuriating!'

'Mmm, good job I'm not the jealous type.' Ian laughed, planting a kiss on his wife's cheek. 'I might start to worry about your interest in the good doctor!'

'You know I only have eyes for you, darling!'

Laura retorted with an ease that spoke volumes about their relationship. 'Still, I'm sure it will come to me eventually where I've seen Niall Gillespie before.'

'Probably just as we're dropping off to sleep to-night,' Ian declared wryly, turning to Sarah and rolling his eyes. 'That's usually how it happens. I'll just be dropping off when she elbows me in the ribs because she's suddenly remembered whatever it was she wanted to tell me. Then she'll immediately go to sleep and I'll be lying there awake all night long!'

They all laughed, Sarah, too, despite the puzzlement she still felt about what had happened just now. It had been extremely odd the way Niall had reacted when Laura had mentioned them having met before. He'd passed it off smoothly enough but she'd sensed that he'd been disturbed by the suggestion. However, she had no chance to think about it any further as Robbie claimed their attention, demanding to hold his lantern as the parade began.

Sarah walked with them as they made their way through the town, Robbie proudly holding his lantern aloft. There was a firework display in the park afterwards and she stayed with Ian and Laura to watch it, although her mind was only partly on what was going on. Her thoughts kept racing ahead to the party later.

Would Niall raise the subject of what had been said in the garden that day? Or would he prefer to forget all about it? It was not knowing that unsettled her but, then, ever since she'd met him she'd been beset by uncertainty.

She sighed as she watched a rocket shoot into the sky in a shower of red and gold sparks. Some day soon she was going to have to work out why Niall had this effect on her. It was just that she had a feeling the answer might bring with it a lot more problems!

It took Sarah longer than she'd expected to get back to where the cars were parked. The crush of bodies was so thick that forging a path through them was nigh on impossible in places. She finally made it, still trying to come up with an excuse to avoid going back to Irene's. Frankly, partying in the company of Niall Gillespie was the last thing she felt like doing at that moment!

'We were just about to give up all hope!' Helen exclaimed as she saw her. 'Irene has gone on ahead with most of the others but we said we'd squeeze you into our car.' Helen shot a dubious glance into the back of the old Volvo. 'It's going to be a tight fit, though. We managed to collect a few more people during the evening.'

'It doesn't matter. Look, Helen, I don't think—' Sarah began, quickly seizing the opening she'd been looking for.

'I'll give Sarah a lift. And anyone else who needs one, of course.'

She swung round at the sound of Niall's voice. She opened her mouth to refuse the offer, but before she could do so Helen spoke up.

'Oh, great! That'll ease things a lot. And there's nobody else to take as we're all sorted now. See you back there, then, folks!'

With a quick wave of her hand Helen jumped

into the car and slammed the door. It shot away to join the long queue making its way from the town. Sarah tried to think of something to say but there was little she could come up with on the spur of the moment. She couldn't refuse the lift without a valid reason for doing so.

'Ready?' Niall unlocked his car and waited for her to join him, giving her little option but to comply. They drove in silence for the first few miles after they finally left the town, Niall concentrating on the heavy traffic, Sarah trying not to concentrate on anything at all. Better to sit there and let her mind go blank rather than risk saying the wrong thing again!

'Look, Sarah, I think we need to sort out a few things, starting with what happened the other day.'

She jumped as he suddenly broke the silence, her heart thundering painfully as she heard what he said.

'I've no idea what you mean,' she began, wanting desperately to avoid any such discussion, but he interrupted her impatiently.

'Of course you have!' he grated out. His face was set in the eerie glow from the dashboard when she cast him a wary glance. 'I owe you an explanation. I realise that. Maybe I should have told you sooner—' he broke off abruptly, leaning forward slightly to peer through the windscreen. 'What the hell is that?'

'What?' Startled, Sarah turned to stare at the road ahead. The night was pitch black now that they had left the town behind. There were no lights along this stretch of road, nothing to dispel the darkness apart from their headlights. She could see nothing at first and then she saw it, a small spot of yellow light dancing crazily about in the middle of the road.

Niall slowed the car to a crawl then slammed on his brakes with a muttered curse when a man appeared slap bang in the beam of their headlights. He was holding a torch, which was what they must have seen waving about in the darkness. He came racing to the car as soon as Niall stopped, panting so hard that it was difficult to understand what he was saying.

'Got…help us. It's…my…wife…'

'Has there been an accident?' Niall demanded, already opening the door to get out. Sarah quickly followed him, frowning as she peered through the darkness. She could just make out the red glow from a car's taillights a couple of hundred yards further on.

'No…no…' The man took a gulping breath and managed to force the words out at last. 'Not an accident, a puncture! And the spare wheel is flat. And my wife is having a baby!'

He turned and started running back along the road, obviously expecting them to follow him.

Niall glanced at Sarah, his brows lifting ruefully. 'Why do I get the impression that he meant that quite literally?'

CHAPTER NINE

'WHAT should we do? I mean, Jenny can't have the baby here by the side of the road!'

Niall smiled reassuringly at the young man who was hovering anxiously around them. 'I'm afraid this baby is coming whether we like it or not! Don't worry, Paul. I've delivered babies under far worse conditions than these, believe me. Now, if you want to do something useful, ring the ambulance control centre again and see if they've got an update on its ETA.'

As Paul hurried over to the car to make the call, Niall turned back to the young woman who was lying on the grass verge. They had arranged a makeshift bed for her out of some old coats and a travel rug which had been in the back of the car. Sarah had angled the torch so that its beam played over the women's lower body and was now busily checking on the baby's progress.

'How are we doing, Sarah?' Niall's voice was utterly composed, betraying not the slightest hint of alarm. She took her lead from him, knowing how important it was that the young mother remained as relaxed as possible. Under these conditions, where there was no possibility of pain relief, they needed Jenny to stay calm.

'Everything is fine, Dr Gillespie. I can see the top of the baby's head now,' she replied with equal composure, although her curiosity had been aroused by his comment. What had he meant when he'd said that he'd delivered babies under far worse conditions?

'Good. It won't be long now, then.' He turned to Jenny, his tone briskly encouraging. 'Now, what I want you to do, Jenny, is to concentrate on everything you've been taught at antenatal classes. You can safely leave the rest to Sarah and me. When I tell you, I want you to pant and try not to push, even though you'll probably want to do so. OK?'

'Yes, I understand.' Jenny managed a smile, although her eyes were scared. 'I think Paul has just about made up for not checking the spare wheel by flagging down you two!'

'Mmm, I imagine the odds on him stopping my car tonight must be several million to one!' Niall laughed then gave his full attention to instructing Jenny how to breathe as another contraction began.

Sarah carefully monitored the baby's progress, nodding as he looked at her. 'Everything's fine,' she assured him in a low voice. 'The baby's head is crowning.'

'It will be another ten minutes yet!' Paul came rushing back to inform them of the ambulance's progress. 'Evidently it's got stuck in traffic leaving Ulverston after the procession.' He dropped down on to the grass beside his wife and took hold of her hand. 'How is she doing? And the baby?'

'Fine. Everything's going—Ah, here we go again!' Niall broke off when Jenny gasped as another contraction hit her. 'Now pant... That's it, nice and steady. Try not to push.'

'Here comes the head.' Sarah felt a thrill of excitement and knew that her tone reflected it. Gently, she supported the baby's head while she ran the tip of her little finger round inside its mouth to clear away any mucus, then laughed as it gave a sudden wail. 'Well, this little one *is* in a hurry to make his presence felt. He can't even wait until he's popped out into the big wide world to have his say!'

Within a few minutes it was all over. Sarah carefully wrapped the baby in the shawl Jenny had packed in her case ready to take to the hospital, then handed the squalling child to its mother. 'A little boy with a fine set of lungs from the sound of it!'

'A boy…' Jenny was laughing and crying at the same time, her fear and pain forgotten as she cradled her baby in her arms. Paul was openly weeping too, his face a mixture of astonishment and pride as he looked at his new son.

'I don't know how to thank you both—' he began, then had to break off as emotion overwhelmed him.

'There's no need for thanks,' Niall said firmly, clapping him on the shoulder. 'We're only too pleased that we were able to help.' He turned to glance along the road as they heard the wail of a siren in the distance, and laughed softly. 'Sounds like the ambulance has made it at last. Still, better late than never, eh?'

Sarah finished covering Jenny and the baby with the rug, then got to her feet and waited by the side of the road as the ambulance drew up. Within a very short time the crew had lifted Jenny and the baby into the back and had made them comfortable. They were just about to shut the doors when Jenny called out.

'Wait a minute, please! Dr Gillespie, what's your first name?'

'Niall,' he replied, sounding rather puzzled by the question.

'Niall,' Jenny repeated, then nodded. 'Yes, I like that.' She glanced at her husband and grinned. 'We couldn't agree on a name, you see, but I think we've just found the perfect one. Is it all right if we name our baby after you, Dr Gillespie?'

'I'd be honoured, Jenny. Thank you,' Niall replied softly with a wealth of emotion in his voice that brought a lump to Sarah's throat.

She blinked back a few tears as they waved the ambulance off, although it was little wonder she was feeling weepy after everything that had happened that night.

'Well, it's been quite an evening, hasn't it? And it isn't over yet.' Niall looked wryly at the muddy patches on the knees of her jeans, then glanced down at his own equally dirty trousers. 'I think we'll have to stop off and get changed before we go on to the party, otherwise we're going to have some explaining to do about how we got into this state!'

Sarah felt herself blush as she heard the teasing note in his voice. She quickly made her way to the car, not allowing herself to think about what interpretation the others might have put on the state of their clothing!

Niall glanced at her as he slid behind the wheel. 'Your place or mine?'

'Pardon?' She flashed him a startled look, seeing the smile that played around his mouth as he started the engine.

'Shall we go to my house first while I get changed or do you want to go to yours?'

'Oh. It…it really doesn't matter,' she finally managed, wondering if she was imagining things. Had she really heard that flirtatious note in his voice just now? she wondered incredulously.

The thought kept her busy for most of the journey, yet by the time they drew up outside his house she still wasn't sure if it had been her imagination, playing tricks again. She cast a quick look round as he cut the engine, wondering if she should offer to wait in the car while he got changed, but he took the decision from her by coming round and opening her door.

Sarah followed him inside the house, waiting while he switched on some lights. He gave her a rueful smile as he glanced at the heaped-up piles of timber and tools spread around the hall.

'I'm having the place renovated so you'll have to excuse the mess. Fortunately, I'm only here to sleep most days so I barely notice it. The kitchen is finished, so do you want to wait in there?'

'Yes, of course.' She picked her way carefully along the hall, then gasped in delight as he thrust open the kitchen door. 'Oh, this is lovely!'

'Do you like it?' Niall followed her into the room and looked around with a satisfied smile. 'I must say that it's turned out exactly how I wanted it to.

When I'm feeling depressed about the state of the place I come in here to remind myself that *maybe* I didn't make a huge mistake, buying this house!'

'Definitely not!' she said with a laugh, unable to hide her delight at the way the room had been fitted out. She ran her fingers lovingly over the knotty old pine from which the cupboards had been built, admiring the craftmanship that had gone into making them. There was even a huge floor-to-ceiling dresser, its shelves laden with yellow and blue pottery which echoed the sunny yellow walls and the simple blue and yellow check curtains that hung at the windows.

Walking over to one of them, she peered out across the garden then jumped when Niall touched her lightly on the arm to draw her attention to where he was pointing.

'There's Adair's flight over there. Can you see it?'

'Y-yes.' She tried to keep her tone as neutral as possible but it wasn't easy to disguise the tremor that ran through the single word. Niall was so close now that she could smell the scent of crushed grass which clung to his clothing, mingled with the clean smell of his skin.

She took a deep breath but that made matters worse rather than better, the fragrances becoming even more potent so that her head swam. The fingers touching her arm lingered for one heartbeat, then two, and she knew that she was holding her breath...Then abruptly Niall moved away.

'I'll just go and get changed. I won't be long. Make yourself some coffee if you fancy some.

You'll find everything you need in the cupboards so just have a root round.'

'Thank you.' Sarah waited until she was sure he'd gone, before turning round. She stared blankly towards the door then took a deep breath, before setting about making the coffee—more for something to do than because she really wanted it. It was better to keep herself busy rather than think about how it had felt when Niall had stood beside her just then.

She found what she needed in the cupboards, then plugged in the coffee maker and turned on the switch. There was a loud bang and the lights suddenly went out, plunging the whole place into darkness.

Sarah pressed a hand to her racing heart, wondering what on earth she had done. She heard Niall calling her name and started towards where she thought the door should be, then cried out in pain as she banged her hip painfully against the corner of the table.

'Sarah! Are you all right?' His voice had taken on a new urgency as soon as he'd heard her cry out. He came racing down the stairs and there was a muttered curse, accompanied by a resounding crash, as he tripped over some of the timber piled up in the hall.

She made her way gingerly to the door, not wanting to risk running into anything else. Her hip was throbbing painfully from the last knock she'd had. 'I'm fine Niall. I don't know what happened. I just switched on the coffee-maker and the lights went out. I'm sorry.'

'Never mind that! Are you sure you're all right?'
He was just a shadow as he came towards her along
the hall. All the lights in the house had gone out so
there was only the silvery wash of moonlight coming through the kitchen windows to see by. It was
only when he arrived in the doorway that she realised he was wearing a pair of jeans and nothing
else.

Her eyes widened as she drank in the sight, her
pupils dilating until the hazel colour almost disappeared. She knew she was staring at him but she
couldn't seem to stop as her gaze travelled over his
leanly muscled torso.

There wasn't an ounce of spare flesh on him, she
realised dizzily as her eyes moved helplessly from
the wide expanse of his muscular shoulders to the
tapering narrowness of his waist. He was like a
sculpture made from solid muscle and bone, his
skin gleaming in the silvery light, the patch of dark
hair that covered his chest tapering to a line which
disappeared beneath the waistband of his jeans. It
was only as she raised her head that she saw the
expression on his face, the way he was looking at
her with a hunger that set every nerve in her body
alight.

'Sarah…' He said her name softly, just as he'd
said it that day by the river, so that for a moment
her head swam as the two scenes merged. She
wasn't sure whether she moved or if he did, but
suddenly his arms were around her and he was
holding her so close that she could feel each and
every one of those muscles imprinting itself against
her softness.

His hand shook just a little as he cupped her cheek to tilt her face for his kiss but, then, she was trembling too. There was magic in that moment, a feeling of anticipation mingled with fear because both of them knew they were stepping over boundaries which had been drawn since that day by the river…and maybe even before then.

Then Niall had kissed her with hunger and need and even passion, but it had been as though he hadn't been able to stop himself from doing so. Now Sarah sensed that he knew exactly what he was doing, that if he'd wanted to he could have and would have stopped. Only he didn't want to stop this time—that was the difference.

As his lips touched hers, gently at first and then with growing urgency, she knew that this kiss was something he wanted as much as she did. It changed everything, erasing the painful memories of that other time, quietening any fears she had. Niall wanted this, he wanted *her*. What was there to be afraid of any more?

'Sarah…Sarah…' He said her name again, repeating it over and over between kisses, turning it into something so beautiful that her eyes filled.

She cradled his face between her hands, kissing him back with every scrap of her being, wanting him to know how much she needed his touch, his kiss. He gave a low groan as he gathered her into his arms, bringing her body into such close contact with his that she was left in little doubt of how he felt at that moment, and her blood raced as she felt her own desire rise to match his.

'Niall.' She whispered his name into the silence,

felt him still as he heard the invitation it held, and her heart missed a beat as she wondered if he would reject what she was offering him...

And then he was bending to lift her into his arms, his mouth taking hers in a drugging kiss as he carried her along the hall and up the stairs.

The bedroom was bare apart from the bed set under the casement window. Niall laid her down gently on the smooth cotton coverlet then lay down beside her. He turned her face towards him and kissed her slowly, tenderly, his lips drawing a response from her which she hadn't known herself capable of before.

Sarah felt the heat of desire gathering in the pit of her stomach, a hot, melting sensation which made her twist restlessly against the cool cotton. The contrast was a sensual stimulant in itself, just as the feel of Niall's cool skin as she ran her hands up his back was—so smooth and cool on the outside, she thought hazily, yet so hot and vibrant beneath!

They made love there on the big old bed with the window wide open to let in the night air. Every touch seemed to be magical, every caress almost unbearably beautiful, so that when they finally became one, Sarah knew that this moment would be imprinted in her mind forever. She had never made love with any man before, had never wanted to, and now she was glad. It was only right that the man she loved with all her heart should be the one to receive this most precious gift.

Dawn came slowly, a pearly shimmer dancing along the horizon to chase away the darkness of the night. Sarah lay on her side, watching as the darkness seeped away and light flowed into the room. She closed her eyes, savouring the memories of the night with greedy delight, remembering every gentle caress, each fervent kiss, the depth of their passion…

'Sarah.'

He said her name softly once again and yet there was something in his voice which made her heart still. Sarah kept her eyes closed as the first cold ripple of fear ran through her body. If Niall regretted what had happened she didn't think she could bear it!

'Oh, Sarah!' He drew her to him, holding her close against the warmth of his body as he kissed her mouth, her cheeks, the hollows of her eyelids, the tiny indentations at her temples.

Sarah trembled with a mixture of relief and desire as he painted her face with kisses of every shade and depth of intensity, as though it were a canvas and he the artist who was bringing it to life. It would be all right! Niall couldn't kiss her this way and regret what had happened…could he? It was that small doubt she couldn't dispel which made her go tense the moment he drew back.

'We need to talk about what happened, Sarah,' he said quietly.

'Why?' She gave a brittle laugh, hearing the strain it held, the uncertainty. 'What is there to talk about, Niall? I don't regret it. I wanted it to happen.' She took her courage in both hands. 'You wanted it, too.'

'Yes, I did!' There was anguish in his agreement, a pain which cut so deeply into her heart that she gasped. She saw his face contort with a sudden spasm of emotion and knew that she couldn't bear to see anything more.

Scrambling out of bed, she searched for something to put on, ashamed now of her nakedness and what it meant. Niall *did* regret making love to her! The realisation cheapened what had been the most precious moment of her life.

'Here.' He handed her a towelling robe, turning away as she drew it on with hands which shook. Picking up his jeans from the heap of clothing on the floor, he dragged them on, before turning to look at her again. In the pale early light his face was all stark angles, his eyes washed free of colour so that they appeared flat and empty.

'I'll make some coffee. No!' He held up his hand when she started to speak. 'It's bad enough that I let this happen. The very least I can do is to explain, Sarah!'

He was gone before she could say anything, the sound of his bare feet padding down the stairs echoing back through the silence. She took a small breath and then another, but her lungs were aching because the air couldn't seem to get inside them. She felt dead and empty and would have given anything just to run from the house and Niall and what he might say. It was only the stark realisation that she couldn't run from her own feelings that stopped her doing so.

No matter what he said or did, it made no difference. She loved him even though he might never feel anything for her...

He was sitting at the kitchen table when she eventually made it downstairs. She'd taken a shower before getting dressed, letting the hot water run down her cold body in the hope that it might warm away the iciness that had invaded her limbs. It hadn't, of course. There was no cure for this chill, or none that was available to her. Niall could make her warm again but she doubted whether what he had to tell her would achieve that!

He got up and poured her a cup of coffee, without saying a word. Sarah sat down unsteadily, contenting herself with warming her hands around the cup because she was afraid to lift it to her lips when her hands were shaking so much.

She heard him utter something rough under his breath but she didn't look at him. She couldn't do that. She couldn't look into his eyes and see the regret there.

'Do you remember last night when I was introduced to Laura?' His voice was low so it wasn't the tone which startled her but the question. She looked up, then quickly looked away again as she found his gaze locked to her face.

'I don't know what you mean,' she said unsteadily.

'Laura said that she thought she recognised me.' His tone was curt, the faint burr it held more pronounced than it had ever been, proof that he wasn't finding this easy either.

She wanted to reach out and touch him, to offer him some measure of comfort no matter how small, but she was afraid of being rebuffed and the repercussions that might have. Her control was very fragile, the slenderest of threads to cling to and face what was to come.

He carried on when she nodded, his voice dropping lower still so that it seemed to grate in the silence and make every nerve in her body hum with tension. 'I didn't know what to say, to be honest. I passed it off because I didn't want to have to admit that she had probably seen a photograph of me and that was why I looked familiar to her.'

'I don't understand. What photograph? What are you saying, Niall?' Suddenly, she knew that she had to know what this was all about. What did Laura and a photograph have to do with any of this?

He stared down at his empty cup and his voice was so bleak that she flinched even before she really grasped what he was saying. 'The one Alison always kept next to her bed. She used to share a room with a girl called Laura when she was a student nurse. It seems more than likely that it was the same Laura we met last night.'

'Alison?' Sarah wet her lips but they felt so parched still that she had trouble speaking. 'Wh-who is Alison?'

He looked up then and his eyes held an expression which seemed to turn her blood to ice. 'My wife.'

CHAPTER TEN

'YOUR wife…?' Sarah could hear the shock in her voice. She stared at Niall, her face as white as the china mug she was cradling between her numb hands.

She took a quick breath as the room swam sickeningly out of focus. It steadied her a little, enough at least to enable her to utter a few more words. 'I…I didn't know you were married.'

'I'm not. Not now.' He got to his feet with an abruptness that made the chair legs scrape against the tiles. Walking over to the window, he rested his hands on the worktop and bowed his head as though suddenly infinitely wearing. 'Alison died three years ago while we were working for the UN in Africa.'

He swung round and Sarah bit her lip as she saw the anguish on his face. 'The baby died with her.'

'Baby…?' She couldn't manage anything more. Her mind was numb from what Niall had told her, her heart aching for the pain she saw on his face. But he didn't appear to need any prompting to continue. She had the feeling that he wanted to tell her—*needed* to tell her—the whole story.

'Yes. Alison was seven months pregnant when she died. It was abruptio placenta.'

'Placental bleeding?' Sarah frowned as she tried to absorb what he was saying. One part of her mind was reeling from the shock, the other part still able to function enough to ask questions. 'But could nothing be done to help her? It isn't usually fatal, surely?'

'If I'd been there maybe I could have done something. That's something I've thought about a million times. Could I have saved Alison?' He ran his hand wearily through his hair. His face was bleak, his eyes clouded with the memory of what had happened. Sarah ached for him and what he was going through, for the pain he felt, but what comfort could she offer him? All she could do was listen to what he was telling her, although her own heart was breaking with despair.

'Where were you, Niall? I know you said you were in Africa, but where were you when…when Alison became ill?'

He sighed heavily as he came and sat down again at the table. 'I'd gone to one of the outlying villages. We were running a vaccination programme in the area at the time. There was a team of us, two doctors and three nurses. Alison was one of the nurses, although she had cut down on the amount of work she was doing as her pregnancy advanced. Oh, she wasn't ill or anything. In fact, she felt marvellous. Being pregnant agreed with her.'

He smiled reminiscently. 'Alison was a very quiet person but very determined in her own way. She refused to return to England when she discovered she was pregnant. She was confident there would be no problem about having the baby where we were living, even though it was a hundred miles or more from the nearest hospital. She persuaded me that it would be all right and that there was nothing to worry about.'

He looked up and Sarah felt her eyes fill as she saw the sorrow on his face. 'I shouldn't have listened to her. I should have made her come back home!'

She touched his hand where it lay on the table. 'You weren't to know, Niall. You couldn't have foretold what was going to happen. Nobody could.'

'Maybe. Maybe not. But at the very least I shouldn't have left her alone for all that time. The village we needed to visit was a day's journey by Jeep from the medical centre. It meant that we would have to travel there the first day, spend the next working, then return on the third. We decided that we'd better all go as there were bound to be other things to attend to as well as the vaccinations. Alison was to remain behind and deal with any minor problems that arose while we were away.'

'So it happened while you were away at this village?' Sarah prompted when he paused.

'Yes. From what I gleaned later, Alison started to bleed heavily during the first afternoon. There were a couple of local women working in the centre with us but they didn't have either the knowledge or experience to know what to do. They made Alison lie down and did the best they could but they couldn't stop the bleeding. A runner was sent to fetch me from the village and I broke all records getting back but it was too late. Alison died from shock brought on by massive blood loss.

'I'm so sorry, Niall. I can't begin to imagine

what you went through.' Sarah brushed away her tears. 'It was a dreadful thing to have happened.'

'But it could have been avoided and that's the worst thing of all, the thing that torments me most. If I hadn't taken Alison out to Africa to work, it would never have happened. God knows, she wasn't the adventurous type! She only went because it was what I wanted to do. I took her out there and yet, when she needed me most of all, where was I? Where was I, Sarah?'

'Don't! Please, don't, Niall!' She got up and went round the table to him. She put her arms around him, holding him close, wanting to comfort him the best way she could. 'It wasn't your fault. You must see that!'

'I wish I could!' He drew back abruptly, making it clear that he didn't want any comfort she might offer him. Sarah stepped back, her hands clenching as she saw the remoteness that settled over his face once again. When he got up and went to the door she didn't try to stop him. How could she? She had nothing to offer him. He might have wanted her physically last night but it wasn't enough to make him forget the woman he still loved.

He paused, with his hand resting on the door handle, and his voice was so empty that her heart almost broke in two. 'Last night should never have happened, Sarah. I blame myself for letting things go that far. It isn't enough to say that I'm sorry, but I am. I only hope that in time you'll be able to forgive me.'

How could she bear it? How could she stand there and listen to him denying everything they'd felt in one another's arms last night…? Only Niall hadn't felt like that. That was what he was telling her. She had been just a substitute for the woman he loved, nothing more.

Sarah didn't know how she managed not to break down at that point. Maybe it was just that she felt numb from what she had learned, she wasn't sure. She drew herself up, her body trembling with the effort it cost her not to let him know how devastated she felt.

'There's nothing to forgive. Now, if you don't mind, I think I would like to go home.' She glanced at the table and her voice wobbled just a little despite her control. 'I…I think it would be better if we both tried to forget this ever happened, don't you?'

He moved aside as she walked to the door. There was a moment when she thought he was going to say something and then it was gone. She led the way through the house and stepped out into the garden, drinking in a deep breath of sweet morning air. The sun was just breaking through the clouds, tendrils of gold settling over the garden. It seemed wrong somehow. It should have been raining, grey and dull, a day to match how she felt, as though all the colour and warmth had suddenly gone from her life.

Niall would never love her as she loved him. It was almost too much to bear!

'Sarah, for heaven's sake, what's the matter with you? The name tags don't match!'

Irene took the baby back to the table and swiftly

cut off the clear plastic bracelet which was fastened around its wrist. Picking up a pen, she filled in another one with the correct details, then fastened it securely and carried the squirming child to its mother.

'Here you are, Mrs Lewis. Would you like to hold Lucy now she's all bathed and beautiful?'

Leaving the excited parents poring over their daughter, Irene went back to finish clearing up. She shot a glance at Sarah, her brows arching teasingly, but Sarah could see the concern in her friend's eyes. 'Making a mistake like that, indeed…and on my last day as well!'

It was all said lightly enough but Sarah knew that it had been unforgivable to make such an error. 'I'm sorry. I…I just didn't realise…'

She broke off as tears welled into her eyes. It had kept happening all the time lately—anything and everything seemed to make her cry. She turned away, barely hearing what Irene said as she quietly instructed Helen to transfer the patient to the wards. Once the door had closed and the room was empty Irene turned back to her again.

'What's wrong, Sarah? Tell me. You haven't been yourself this past week, not since the night of my party, in fact. What really happened then? Oh, I know that you and Niall Gillespie got caught up, assisting at that roadside birth, but something else went on, didn't it?'

'I don't know what you mean.' Sarah tried to laugh off the question but it sounded too shrill, verging on hysteria. She bit her lip as she busied herself with clearing up the delivery room ready for the next patient.

'Don't you?' Irene gave her a level look. 'I'm not blind, you know. I know something went on between you and Niall Gillespie that night.' She saw the startled glance Sarah shot her and smiled kindly. 'You'd have to be deaf, dumb and blind not to notice how edgy you are around him, love! Is there something going on with you two I should know about?'

'Hardly!' Sarah modified her tone as she saw Irene's start of surprise. She gave a small shrug, affecting amusement. 'I don't think there's any danger of Niall being interested in me, Irene.'

'But how about you? Are you interested in him?' Irene didn't wait for her to reply but tactfully changed the subject, for which Sarah was grateful. Somehow she got through the rest of the morning without making any more mistakes but it was an effort to concentrate on her work just as it was an effort to concentrate on anything at the moment. Her mind kept returning time and again to what had happened, to that one glorious night when the world had seemed to be hers and to the following morning when it had all crumbled around her.

By the time lunchtime came she was near despair. Nothing would change the fact that Niall was still in love with his wife. She had to accept that and get on with her own life, but suddenly she knew that it would be impossible while she saw him each day. She had to make the break and leave Dalverston General. It was the only way she would

ever be free from the agony of knowing how little
Niall really cared for her.

Leaving her lunch in her locker, Sarah went to
the hospital library and took a stack of nursing jour-
nals off a shelf. There were plenty of jobs on offer,
ranging from community midwifery to a position
with a private practice in London. She photocopied
the relevant pages and put them in her bag to be
dealt with when she got home that night. It wasn't
that she wanted to leave Dalverston, but what
choice did she have? Seeing Niall day after day, it
was too much to cope with.

As though to prove that point, she was brought
into contact with him that very afternoon when an
emergency case was rushed in. Sarah went to meet
the ambulance as it roared into the bay, her heart
going out to the woman who was lying unconscious
on the stretcher. The ambulance crew had attached
a saline drip to her arm and Sarah held the door
wide open so that it wouldn't snag on the line as
the paramedics brought the patient inside.

'What have we got?' she asked.

'Her name is Teresa Kelly. Severe vaginal bleeding. That's all we know so far, apart from the fact
that she had a baby a couple of weeks ago. A and
E is snowed up with cases so the control centre said
to bring her straight here.'

The paramedic glanced over his shoulder as a car
roared up to the door. 'That'll be the husband. He
had to drop the other kids off at a relative's house
before he could come here. There are five little
ones, all under the age of seven, I gather. Plus the

baby, which makes a grand total of six,' the paramedic informed her dryly.

'Six?' Sarah shot a startled glance at the unconscious woman. 'She doesn't look old enough!'

'You said it!' The paramedic didn't say anything
more as they got on with transferring Teresa Kelly
onto a trolley. With the aid of one of the porters,
Sarah took her straight upstairs to surgery then instructed Helen to take the woman's blood pressure
and pulse while she rang through for a doctor. She
expected Meena to attend the call but when the door
opened it was Niall who had responded.

'Meena is busy. What have we got?'

His tone was curt, his attention focused solely on
the patient, who was still unconscious. Sarah took
a deep breath, forcing herself to concentrate on her
as well, although being near Niall again wasn't the
easiest thing to handle.

'Her name is Teresa Kelly and she had a baby
about two weeks ago. Evidently it was her sixth
child. There's severe vaginal bleeding, but we don't
know anything else as yet,' she informed him quietly.

'Why not? For heavens sake, Sarah, surely you
know enough by now to get the patient's history so
we have some idea what we're dealing with?' He
turned to Helen, his tone icily controlled. 'Go and
see if you can find her notes and get them back
here as fast as you can.'

He turned a cold green stare on Sarah as Helen
hurried towards the door. 'Did anybody come in
with her?' he demanded.

'He—her husband should be downstairs by now,'

she replied shakily, trying not to let him see how much it hurt to have him speak to her in that sharp manner.

She turned away as he curtly instructed Helen to see what she could find out from Teresa's husband as well, her hands shaking as she quickly removed the woman's bloodsoaked underclothing. Did Niall feel so guilty about what had happened that he was blaming her for it now? It seemed the only explanation.

'Right, let's see what we can find.' His expression was grim as he set about examining the unconscious woman. 'What's her blood pressure and temperature like?'

Sarah picked up the chart and quickly gave him the readings. He nodded briefly, concentrating on what he was doing. He had almost finished his examination when Teresa Kelly started to come round.

'Where am I?' She struggled to sit, then doubled up in pain and clutched her stomach.

'Just lie still, Mrs Kelly.' Niall eased the ashen-faced woman back against the pillows and frowned in concern. 'When did this all start? Have you been bleeding heavily since your last child was delivered?'

'Yes, quite heavily. I thought it would stop but it's got worse this past day or so. And then I started to feel sort of feverish and dizzy. That's when the pain started—just here.' Teresa gingerly touched her abdomen. Beads of perspiration were forming on her brow and Sarah moved quietly to the head of the bed to wipe them away.

'And were there any complications during the birth?' Niall queried. 'I've sent a nurse to find your notes, but if you could just fill me in, Mrs Kelly, it would save time.'

'No. It…it was all simple enough,' Teresa muttered, carefully avoiding his eyes as she stared at her hands, which were still tightly pressed against her stomach.

'I see.' It was obvious that he had caught the reluctance in her voice. Sarah wondered what was behind it, but before she could speculate further Niall turned to her, his manner once more brusquely professional.

'I think I need to take a closer look to see if I can spot what's causing this. Get the patient ready, please, Staff.'

Sarah did as she'd been requested, helping Teresa out of her clothes and into a disposable gown while Niall scrubbed up. Helen came back while they were doing that and went straight over to him, lowering her voice so that only he could hear what she was saying. However, Sarah could tell from the low imprecation he uttered that he wasn't pleased with what he'd learned.

His face was set as he beckoned her to join them. 'Evidently, Mrs Kelly wasn't admitted to hospital for the birth of her last child. Nor did she have a midwife in attendance. According to the husband, his mother delivered the baby.'

'His mother? Is she trained for such things?' Sarah asked, unable to hide her dismay.

'No.' Niall's tone was harsh. 'It seems that the husband can't see any point in making a fuss about something as trivial as having a baby. It's what a woman is made for so she may as well get on with it, or words to that effect.'

'Good heavens! You can't believe anyone would take that view nowadays.' Sarah glanced back at the young woman lying on the bed and her face softened in sympathy. 'Maybe that explains why she's had so many children in such a short space of time. Her husband probably doesn't believe in contraception either.'

'Probably not.' There was a grating quality to Niall's voice all of a sudden. She glanced at him and was shocked by the bitterness she saw on his face. She longed to know what was causing it but there was no way she dared ask him with Helen standing there, listening.

She kept her mind on the job with a determined effort of will. 'So it's possible that Teresa's illness has something to do with the lack of proper medical care during the birth of her last child.'

'It's more than possible. I'd say that was the root cause. It wouldn't surprise me if pieces of the placenta were left behind and they've set up an infection in the womb. The signs are all indicative of that, from the excessive bleeding to the pain and fever. She'll be lucky if she isn't suffering from toxaemia as well. We'll have to do blood tests but the most important thing now is to find out exactly what's going on inside her.'

He moved away, leaving her and Helen to scrub up. Sarah went back to assist him, trying to keep her mind solely on what was happening. She would think about what had been behind that expression on his face later, when she was alone. One thing she was certain of was that he wouldn't welcome her interest!

'Just try a sip of this, Teresa...good. Once those antibiotics start to work you'll feel a lot better. Dr Gillespie has removed all the placental debris but there's still a lot of infection inside you which must be cleared up.'

'Thank you. I've given everyone a lot of trouble, haven't I?' Teresa smiled wanly. She would be quite pretty, Sarah thought, if she didn't look so washed-out. Her face was far more lined than it should have been for her age, but it was only to be expected. Being mother to six young children couldn't be easy.

'Of course you aren't being any trouble! Don't be silly. We just want you to get better. Then you'll be able to go back home to your family,' she said encouragingly as she put the glass down on the locker, but Teresa turned away.

'I wish I didn't have to go back!' The woman bit back a sob. 'I don't know if I can take any more! I never seem to have a moment to myself, what with the cooking and the cleaning and all the washing for the kids.'

'Isn't there anyone who would help you?' Sarah suggested. 'A friend or relative, perhaps?'

'Who wants to help look after six kids?' Teresa rubbed her eyes with the back of her hand. 'No, there's no one but Lee's mother, and she's too busy looking after her own family. In her view, I should just get on with it and stop complaining!'

'It must be hard, though. Six children are a lot for anyone to cope with,' Sarah replied, wondering how to put the suggestion delicately. 'Maybe you should think about some permanent method of contraception if you don't want to add to your family. You could be sterilised, Teresa. Or, simpler still, your husband could have a vasectomy. It's a fairly minor procedure for a man, you know.'

Teresa laughed bitterly. 'I can just see Lee agreeing to that—I don't think! In his view, the more kids we have the more it goes to prove how wonderful he is. The doctor warned me after the fifth baby that I shouldn't have any more, but Lee took no notice.'

'Then perhaps you should do something about it yourself, Teresa. It's your body, after all, and your life. You can't leave the decisions up to someone else, especially when it appears they don't have your welfare at heart.' She gave the woman a moment to absorb that, then smiled at her and left before she said anything she shouldn't. It was hard to believe that any woman would allow herself to be so downtrodden in this day and age...

'I'd like a word with you, Sarah, if you have a minute.'

She came to a halt, her heart hammering, as Niall suddenly appeared. He led the way to the office without waiting for her agreement, stepping aside for her to precede him into the room. Closing the door, he leaned back against it as he studied her closely. Sarah had the impression that something was troubling him deeply and her heart raced faster than ever.

Surely he wasn't having a sudden change of heart about the other night, was he?

'I need to speak to you about what happened at my house.'

The words only seemed to strengthen the idea so that she went momentarily giddy with anticipation. Her voice was slightly breathless when she spoke.

'What about it, Niall?' she said softly.

'About what we did, and what could happen as a result of us letting our...desires get the better of us!' He ran a hand through his hair in a gesture of impatience. 'You must know what I'm getting at, Sarah, for heavens sake!'

She did. She also understood what she had seen on his face earlier, that look of bitterness and self-reproach. She felt an urge to laugh but it was just a cover for the pain she felt as she was forced to accept just how *much* he regretted what had happened that night, not to mention any possible repercussions there might be!

'Don't worry, Niall. I'm quite sure I'm not pregnant, if that's what you're worried about! I suggest you put what happened right out of your mind.' She gave a bitter laugh, hurt beyond belief by what he had just said. 'After all, everyone is entitled to the odd lapse...even you!'

She walked deliberately to the door. Niall hesitated for a moment, making her wonder if there was something else he wanted to say. But he finally stepped aside without uttering a word. Sarah left the office on leaden legs, her heart aching. If she'd been holding out any hopes that he might change his mind, that episode had destroyed them completely.

She couldn't face seeing anyone at that moment so she went to the day room, which was empty at this hour when most of the mums were resting before evening visiting began. Walking to the window, she stared out across the town, feeling more alone than she had felt in the whole of her life as the situation suddenly became crystal clear.

She had given her heart to a man who had no use for it. There was only one woman Niall had wanted, just one woman he'd wanted to bear his children. And it wasn't her!

CHAPTER ELEVEN

'THERE'll be nobody left soon! First Dr Henderson, then Irene and now you!' Sally slammed her locker door and glared at Sarah. 'I never thought you'd leave!'

'Neither did I. But it was just too good an opportunity to miss.' Sarah closed her locker and smiled, although there was a heavy weight in her heart. Making the decision to leave Dalverston, it hadn't been easy, despite knowing that it was the right thing to do.

'Private midwifery, though?' Sally frowned. 'Seems a strange idea to me, but I suppose it's no different from any other form of private health care.'

'Exactly. And it promises to be interesting, working both in the clinic and in people's own homes. I'm really looking forward to it. Anyway, things are bound to change around here once the new extension is built,' she said encouragingly when Sally still looked dubious.

'I suppose so. But it won't be the same!'

Sally led the way from the staffroom, leaving Sarah to follow. Sarah sighed as she made her way to the office to report for duty. It wouldn't be the same and it probably wouldn't be better either. But it wouldn't be worse, and that was all she was trying to avoid!

Working here with Niall, it had reached the point where it had become almost intolerable. It didn't matter that he treated her with the same distant courtesy as he treated the rest of the staff. There was too much between them to go back to the beginning and return to being colleagues. Maybe Niall could blot what had happened from his mind but she couldn't! The memory of that night in his arms haunted her still.

'Right, that's about it, then.' Brenda Carlisle, the sister who had been on duty all day, finished giving Sarah a run-down on what had happened and any problems she needed to watch out for. 'I hope you have a quiet night. By the way, I heard on the grapevine that you've handed in your notice and are heading for the bright city lights.'

'That's right. I leave at the end of the month,' Sarah agreed as she finished making notes about what needed to be done.

'I'm surprised, I must say. I thought you'd be taking over from Irene. You must be in the running for her job?'

She shrugged. 'Maybe. But I felt like a change.'

'Oh, well, if that's the way you feel, better to go now rather than later, eh?'

Brenda left soon after that and Sarah set about seeing what needed to be done. With Irene having gone and no replacement as yet, the job of supervising the other staff had fallen to her. It was a quiet night, luckily enough, with just one admission soon after visiting hours had finished.

She made sure that the outer doors were locked after the last visitor left, before going back to the wards. For security reasons they were always kept locked after evening visiting was over, any incoming patients needing to ring the bell for admittance. There had never been a problem in the unit but she knew that both the staff and the mums felt happier knowing the building was secure.

After making certain that everything was sorted out, she made her way to the delivery room where Helen and Sally were both assisting at a birth.

'Everything all right here?' she asked quietly.

'Fine. Mrs Davies is expecting her husband to arrive once he gets the message she's left for him. He's at a church meeting,' Sally advised her.

'I'll listen out for the bell,' Sarah assured her, then left them to it. She went back down the corridor and made a quick check on all the wards, stopping to chat to several of the mums along the way. A few were watching television in the day room but most were lying on their beds, reading or chatting. There was no strict regime about when the lights went out but most were glad to settle down around ten o'clock.

Giving birth was an exhausting process and most women valued their time in hospital as a chance to rest, before going home and picking up the threads of often hectic lives.

Assured that everything was as it should be, Sarah made her way to the office to sort out some paperwork which had mounted up during the day. The door was closed when she got there and she was surprised to find that the lights had been turned off as well.

She felt along the wall for the switch and turned

them back on, then gasped in surprise as she suddenly spotted a man by the drugs cupboard. There was a moment when her mind tried to make sense of what she was seeing. Had someone let Mrs Davie's husband in and shown him in here? But why would he be in the dark if that was the case?

He suddenly turned round and she gasped again as she recognised him. 'Gary! What on earth—?' she began, but got no further as he raced across the room towards her. She had no chance of getting out of the way as he gave her a violent shove which sent her flying. Her head connected with the edge of the desk with a sickening crunch, then everything went dark.

The light was making her head hurt. Sarah turned away from the bright glow, then groaned as the action made her head pound sickeningly. She was vaguely aware of a movement beside her and a cool hand touched her cheek.

'Sarah? Can you hear me, sweetheart?'

She recognised Niall's voice but not the words he said, that softly tender endearment. She clamped her eyes tightly shut against a pain which was even worse than the one inside her head as she fought to control her imagination. Niall wasn't here! It was just her mind, playing tricks...

'Sarah, speak to me. Anything. Tell me to go away but just say something so I'll know that you're all right!'

There was such anguish in his voice that her eyes flickered open despite her reluctance. Carefully, she turned her head on the pillow and felt her heart lurch to an unsteady stop as she found Niall bending over her. There was such anxiety in his eyes, such concern, such…

She bit her lip, afraid to let the word slip into her thoughts because of the pain it could cause. 'Wh-what happened?' she murmured huskily instead.

'Don't you remember?' He sounded even more concerned, his green eyes shimmering with such emotion she felt dazzled by it. She closed her eyes again, afraid of what her foolish mind was conjuring up in its confused state. Niall didn't feel for her what she felt for him—he'd made that abundantly clear!

Her brow wrinkled as she tried to piece together the hazy images floating around inside her head and remember what had happened—darkness, a sudden flare of light, a figure racing towards her…

She gasped as the jigsaw fitted together at last. 'It was Gary! You know who I mean, Trisha's Gary. He was in the office and he pushed me. But…but what was he doing there?'

'What do you think?' Niall's tone was grim as he straightened abruptly. A veil seemed to fall over his face all of a sudden, concealing the warmth and emotion she'd seen there for those few fleeting moments. Sarah struggled to contain an overwhelming sense of loss. She'd known it had been her imagination playing tricks, but it still hurt to see the proof of that all the same.

'He was after drugs, of course. He must have discovered where they were kept when he came into the unit to visit Trisha. If you recall, Ariel was on diazepam at the time. I imagine Gary heard someone mention it and that sparked the idea of trying to steal it from here. There's a big market for diazepam on the streets.'

'Drugs…?' she repeated blankly. She stared at him in shock, then gasped as she suddenly recalled something else. 'I caught Trisha in the office early one morning just before she was discharged. Do you think she might have been checking to see what she could find?'

'Probably. I imagine Gary made her do it. You know how under his thumb she was, but that's no excuse.' Niall's tone was unyielding. 'I'll ring the police and let them know anyway. They'll want to speak to her, I imagine.'

'So you knew it was Gary, did you?' she asked, wincing as she tried to ease herself up against the pillows.

'Lie still! You've got one hell of a bump on your head.' He came and sat down on the edge of the bed, taking care not to jolt it. He studied her wan face for a moment, his eyes lingering on the huge bruise on her left temple while a look of fury contorted his features. 'I only wish I could get my hands on that louse…'

'It's probably better that you can't!' She managed a laugh, although her heart was drumming like crazy, making her head ache even more with the pressure. Niall looked so angry and all because she had been hurt! Surely that must mean he felt something for her? she reasoned, trying to control the elation she felt at the idea.

'Probably.' His tone was wry as he took her hand and held it gently between both of his. He didn't seem to notice the tremor that ran through her as he absently smoothed her fingers. 'Anyway, there isn't much likelihood of that happening because the police have Gary in custody.'

'Th-that was quick.' Sarah wondered if he would attribute the quaver in her voice to what had happened—until she saw the look he shot her. He let go of her hand and stood up abruptly.

'We have Mike Dawson to thank for that. Evidently, when Gary found that he couldn't get out through the street doors he tried making a run for it via the main building. Mike happened to spot him coming out of the unit and challenged him.' Niall shrugged, carefully avoiding her eyes as he moved away from the bed. 'They had a bit of tussle evidently, but Mike came out on top in the end.'

'That was f-fortunate,' she said, closing her eyes so that he couldn't see how it hurt to have him turn away from her like that. 'I...I think I'd like to rest now, if you don't mind, Niall,' she whispered brokenly, unable to take any more of this torment in her present state.

'Of course. I'm sorry. I didn't mean to—' He bit off the rest of what he'd been going to say. Walking to the door, he paused with his hand on the knob, and there was a grating quality to his voice which made her eyes open. 'If there's anything you need, let me know, please, Sarah. Promise?'

The irony was almost too bitter to bear. The only thing she needed was the one thing she could never have—him! She didn't say anything in reply, closing her eyes again as he left the room. Any physical pain she felt came a poor second to the nagging ache inside her. She loved Niall with all her heart and always would. How pointless it was!

'I'm fine, honestly! Look, Laura, I really appreciate your offer but I don't need any nursing!' Sarah struggled to inject an airy note into her voice as her friend immediately began to protest. 'No, no, and no again! You have enough to do without coming round here to look after me. Anyway, Irene said that she'd pop round later so I won't be on my own.'

It was just a small distortion of the truth after all. Irene had rung and offered to visit but Sarah had put her off, just as she intended to put Laura off. She sighed as she was finally able to end the call. Everyone had been so kind, offering to look after her, but all she wanted was to be left on her own.

She had spent the past two days in hospital, trying to put a brave face on things, but now she just wanted to be alone. It wasn't the mild concussion or the bruises that were bothering her. What ailed her most was far more serious. A broken heart was something she would never fully recover from, but somehow she had to deal with it and get on with her life.

Niall didn't love her but the world hadn't come to an end just because he had made that clear, although sometimes it felt as though it had!

He hadn't come to see her again while she'd been in the ward and she hadn't been surprised. He'd done his duty, by visiting her, and that had been it. Had he found out about her handing in her notice yet? she wondered suddenly. She almost laughed out loud. Why should he care? She was doing both of them a favour by leaving. Niall wouldn't need to be constantly reminded of the lapse he'd had, and she wouldn't be constantly thinking about how much he regretted making it!

Moodily, Sarah wandered around the house, trying to find something to take her mind off all the maudlin thoughts that filled it. Elaine Roberts, the hospital manager, had insisted she take sick leave for the rest of the week and the days spread emptily ahead of her. She'd wanted desperately to be by herself but, perversely, now that she was on her own she felt so lonely she could have wept!

In an effort to distract herself she decided to make a start on sorting out what she wanted to take with her to London. She would need to hire a removal van to deal with her furniture, but there were ornaments and china and all the usual clutter she'd accumulated in the past few years. It all needed to be sorted through and any rubbish thrown out, but after just half an hour she felt too restless to remain in the house any longer.

The weather had changed that day, a cool breeze blowing down from the hills and lowering the temperature by several degrees. She found her quilted jacket and zipped it up, before setting out for a walk in the hope that it would ease her restlessness. Once again she made her way to the river and stood on the bank, watching the grey water rushing past her feet. She didn't even realise that she was crying until she felt the wetness on her cheeks. Once she left Dalverston that would be the end of everything.

She would never see Niall again. How could she bear it?

'Don't cry, my darling.'

His voice cut through her unhappy thoughts, bringing her swinging round so fast she almost lost her footing on the slippery bank. Niall reached out and grabbed her, bringing her hard against him and holding her there so that she could feel the heavy beating of his heart under her palms.

'Seems to me that you need someone to take care of you, Staff Nurse Harris.'

His tone was meant to be light but it failed miserably. Sarah felt every nerve in her body go taut. She took a tiny breath, far too small to inflate her lungs but big enough to enable her to ask a question. 'Is…is that an offer, Dr Gillespie?'

He gave a deep laugh, so soft and sensuous that each and every one of her nerve endings flared to life, sending tiny electric charges pulsing through her skin. 'Yes, it is! Seems to me it's way past time I made it, too.'

'Niall!' His name was swallowed up by the hungry assault of his mouth as he bent and kissed her. Sarah clung to him, feeling the familiar warmth of his body beneath her hands. The joy which filled her heart so great that she thought it would burst.

She kissed him back with the same hunger, the same need, the same tenderness, smiling when he drew back, his eyes as dazed as she knew hers must be. 'I love you, Sarah! I've been the biggest fool imaginable not to realise it sooner, but I love you!'

'And I love you, Niall.' She drew his head down as she stared into his stormy green eyes, letting him see that she meant every word. 'I love you more than I thought it possible to love anyone.'

'Darling!' His mouth was even hungrier this time, his passion barely held in check so that her head swam. He drew her to him and held her close so that even through the thickness of their clothing she was in little doubt of how much he wanted her. Sarah had no idea what might have happened next if they hadn't both become aware of children's voices, shouting excitedly.

Niall's face was wry as he let her go and glanced towards the playground, where a gaggle of children were squabbling over who should have first go on the swings. 'Hmm, this seems just a little too public for what I have in mind. How close is your house, Sarah?'

'Oh, close enough!' She grinned as she slipped her hand into his and they turned to walk back up the path. They skirted the playground and Niall paused, a faint wistfulness creeping over his face as he looked at the children.

'Maybe one day, Sarah, our child will be in there, playing,' he said quietly.

It was everything she could have hoped for, the sweetest kind of promise, a pledge of total commitment. She reached up and kissed him on the cheek, feeling her heart fill that little bit more. 'I'd say that was more probable than possible, darling.'

Hand in hand they walked back to her house. Sarah let them in then closed the door and stepped into his arms. His kiss was even more urgent than before, his hunger and need for her rising to new heights, but hers rose to meet it without any hesitation. She wanted him as much as he wanted her. He was her light, her warmth, her life…her reason for being.

They made love in her room, the narrow restrictions of the single bed no hindrance to their passion. Each kiss and caress was more beautiful, more potent than the last so that she was trembling with desire when Niall shed his clothing and lay down beside her.

He held her face between his hands and stared into her eyes with so much love that a lump closed her throat. 'I love you, Sarah Harris. I love you more than I have ever loved any other woman.'

'Even…even Alison?' she whispered shakily, barely able to believe what he was saying.

He kissed her with slow languor, his body making its own blatant statement of how he felt. 'Yes, even more than Alison. Alison and I grew up together. What I felt for her was something entirely different. I loved her but I don't think I was *in love* with her. I know it never felt like this…'

His mouth claimed hers then, the drugging kiss closing her mind to everything else as he made love to her with a fiery intensity and need which drove them both to dizzying heights.

Sarah clung to him as the world spun off its axis. He was all she needed in her life, all she would ever want…just Niall and his love!

'Whoever invented single beds should be shot!' Niall groaned dramatically as he tried to ease his rangy frame into a more comfortable position.

Sarah laughed as she kissed his chin. 'Single beds are made for single people. It's been perfectly fine up to this point, I assure you!'

'Mmm, well, I won't argue with that. It's nice to know that there has been only you in it all by yourself up till now.' He didn't attempt to disguise the possessive note in his voice and she felt her heart lift again. He returned her kiss, his just a little longer and more thorough than hers had been so that she moaned softly as he drew back.

He laughed at the expression on her face and kissed the tip of her nose. 'How about a king-sized bed when we get married? Think that's too big or what?'

'I... You...' She took a deep breath but her voice was still rather squeaky. 'Was that a proposal, Dr Gillespie?'

'Yes.' He lifted an arrogant brow. 'I think I know the answer already but I suppose it's only right to hear you accept.'

'Why, you...you conceited wretch!' She aimed a punch at his shoulder then squealed as he scooped her to him and held her so close that she could barely breathe, let alone aim a second blow.

'Yes or no? Come on, make up your mind,' he ordered, rubbing his chin against her cheek so that the faint rasp of beard made a shiver dance through her body, which, of course, he felt. His smile was even smugger, if that were possible. 'Will you or won't you marry me?'

'Well, if it will stop you acting the caveman...!' Sarah sighed theatrically. 'I suppose it will have to be yes!'

'Good. Although, in all fairness, I have to tell you that I had no intention of taking no for an answer. I meant to persuade you…by fair means or foul.'

The sensuous note in his deep voice made her tremble. 'Mmm, makes me wish I'd held out a bit longer,' she confessed with a shaky laugh.

'Oh, don't worry. You're now in line for a reward for not keeping me waiting. Whichever way you look at it, Sarah, you can't lose.'

There was faint uncertainty in his voice suddenly, and she propped herself up on one elbow to look at him. 'The only way I could possibly lose is if you didn't love me, Niall.'

'But I do. I think I've been in love with you for a long time, ever since that day I kissed you beside the river. I…I was just afraid to face up to how I felt because I was so guilty about it,' he confessed quietly.

'Because of Alison?'

'Yes,' he sighed as he drew her into his arms and held her close. 'It didn't seem right that I should find love and happiness again when she had died. I felt so guilty about it happening because if I hadn't taken Alison to Africa and let her get pregnant, she would still be alive today. I swore to myself that never again would I put any woman in that position, that I preferred to steer clear of any personal involvement rather than take that risk again.'

'But it wasn't your fault, Niall!' she said, hating to hear him say such things. She tilted her head back so that she could look into his face, and was glad to see him smile in acceptance.

'I realise that now, but before I met you I never allowed myself to think about what had happened rationally. It wasn't hard because there was never a need to do so. Until you came into my life, Sarah, I was content to remain on my own for the rest of my life with only my work to keep me company.

'I knew you were dangerous to my equilibrium from the first time I set eyes on you in the staffroom that day, but I was determined to fight my feelings because I felt so guilty.'

'I thought it was because you were still so in love with Alison that you couldn't bear the thought of another woman in your life,' she admitted quietly, and felt him tense as he heard the catch in her voice.

'No! It was true, what I said before—I loved Alison. She'd always been a part of my life and she was a gentle, sweet girl. But I never loved her as I love you, Sarah. It wasn't because I couldn't love you as much as Alison, but because I knew just how much I *could* love you! It made me feel as guilty as hell to realise it so that's why I decided that we should end things.'

'I see. But what made you change your mind, then?' she asked, smiling as he smoothed the tiny furrows from between her brows with a gentle finger.

'Hearing that you'd handed in your notice, that's what! It suddenly hit me that you were going to walk out of my life for good and I'd never see you again. I think I was already starting to come to my senses after you were hurt, but it took that to jolt me into action and make me see what I was allowing to happen.'

He grinned, looking both boyishly handsome and so wickedly sexy so that Sarah's pulse leapt. 'There was a planning meeting this afternoon but I sent my apologies to the Board and explained that I had something urgent to attend to and came straight here! And it wasn't a lie. Making love to you was a very pressing need which had to be attended to—urgently!'

Her delighted gurgle of laughter changed to a moan of passion as his mouth found the tip of her breast. She closed her eyes as she felt the fierce rush encompass her totally. Niall was right—there was nothing quite so urgent as love!

EPILOGUE

'AND now we come to the point in the evening you've all been waiting for—the winner of this year's competition to deliver the most babies.' Dr Henderson, who had been invited back to do the honours at the staff Christmas dinner, smiled around the room. 'And it goes to Sarah Gillespie…again!'

Sarah smiled as a loud burst of applause rang out around the room. Niall leaned over and kissed her on the cheek, his eyes adding his own adoring congratulations as she got up and went to receive her award—a decidedly drunken-looking wooden stork, carrying a baby in its beak!

'Well done, Sarah. Two years on the run, eh?' Dr Henderson patted her on the shoulder. 'Going to try to make it a hat trick, my dear?'

Sarah smiled as she looked around the room at the people she knew so well. Irene gave her a broad wink, making her wonder if somehow she suspected…

She took a deep breath as her gaze made its way back to Niall, who was watching her with such love in his eyes that she felt her heart swell. They had been married two months now, two gloriously happy months which she'd thought couldn't be bettered. But suddenly she knew that the best was still to come!

'Thank you all very much for this.' She waited until the ripple of applause had died down, before continuing, her eyes locked to Niall's. 'However, I don't think I shall be in the running for next year's award, although I promise to contribute to it in some small way. Where else would I chose to have my own baby but right here at Dalverston General?'

There was a moment's stunned silence before everyone laughed in delight. Sarah accepted the congratulations that were showered on her as she made her way back to her table, but her eyes were still locked to Niall's face as she watched the rapid play of emotions which crossed it in swift succession.

He rose to his feet and swept her into his arms, ignoring the cheer that went up as he kissed her soundly. He finally let her go and Sarah was touched to see the glimmer of tears in his eyes even though he smiled at her.

'You wretch, Sarah Gillespie. Fancy springing it on me like that!' He took a deep breath, his eyes saying everything he couldn't with so many people listening.

'I think this is as good a time as any to leave, don't you?' she suggested with a wicked little grin.

She turned to lead the way from the room, then paused as Sally caught her eye and winked. 'Remember what I said about TLC, Sarah? It's worked a treat!'

Sarah laughed as she carried on, although once outside in the corridor she had to wait a few moments for Niall to catch up with her.

'Everyone wanted to offer their congratulations!'

he explained with a grin as he took her arm and
guided her into an alcove well away from any pry-
ing eyes. He bent and kissed her again with highly
satisfying thoroughness, then drew back with a
frown. 'What was that Sally said, by the way?'

Sarah reached up and wiped a smudge of lipstick
off his mouth with a smug smile. 'Oh, nothing
much. It was that just a while ago she said something about you needing a good woman to give you
a bit of TLC, that's all.'

He laughed throatily. 'I don't know about a *good*
woman after that scam you just pulled! But the TLC
sounds good to me.' He punctuated each word with
kisses. 'Tender…loving…care. What more could
any man ask for? But, then, what more could any
man want when he has you?'

'Our baby,' she suggested softly, nestling against
him as his arms enfolded her.

'That's going to be the most wonderful bonus of
all,' Niall replied before his mouth found hers once
again. 'You and our child, Sarah… I couldn't wish
for anything more!'

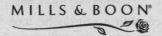

MILLS & BOON®

Enchanted™

THE SHEIKH'S REWARD by Lucy Gordon

Frances wanted an interview with Sheikh Ali Ben Saleem, and he agreed—on condition she accompany him to his kingdom. Once there, however, Frances found herself imprisoned by his concubines! What was more…Ali was insisting on marriage…

BRIDE ON LOAN by Leigh Michaels

Caleb Tanner needs a decoy to save him from the many women scheming to get him to the altar! Sabrina isn't thrilled about moving in with Caleb. He's too attractive for his own good. He's also her agency's biggest client so she has no choice but to play the bride-to-be.

HONEYMOON HITCH by Renee Roszel

Jake has made it clear that he wants children from his marriage of convenience with Susan. Yet, while Susan yearns for Jake's love without having even experienced a kiss from him, the most daunting thing on the horizon isn't their wedding day…but their wedding night!

A WIFE AT KIMBARA by Margaret Way

Brod Kinross suspects Rebecca of being a gold-digger, after his father's money. In fact it's not the money that Rebecca wants—or Brod's father—it's love and marriage to Brod himself…

Available from 5th May 2000

Available at most branches of WH Smith, Tesco, Martins, Borders, Easons, Volume One/James Thin and most good paperback bookshops

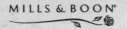

4 FREE

books and a surprise gift!

We would like to take this opportunity to thank you for reading this Mills & Boon® book by offering you the chance to take FOUR more specially selected titles from the Medical Romance™ series absolutely FREE! We're also making this offer to introduce you to the benefits of the Reader Service™—

★ FREE home delivery
★ FREE gifts and competitions
★ FREE monthly Newsletter
★ Exclusive Reader Service discounts
★ Books available before they're in the shops

Accepting these FREE books and gift places you under no obligation to buy, you may cancel at any time, even after receiving your free shipment. Simply complete your details below and return the entire page to the address below. *You don't even need a stamp!*

YES! Please send me 4 free Medical Romance books and a surprise gift. I understand that unless you hear from me, I will receive 6 superb new titles every month for just £2.40 each, postage and packing free. I am under no obligation to purchase any books and may cancel my subscription at any time. The free books and gift will be mine to keep in any case.

M0EA

Ms/Mrs/Miss/Mr ....Initials.....................................
BLOCK CAPITALS PLEASE

Surname ....

Address ....

....

....Postcode....................................

Send this whole page to:
UK: FREEPOST CN81, Croydon, CR9 3WZ
EIRE: PO Box 4546, Kilcock, County Kildare (stamp required)

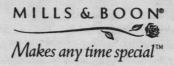